SWEET TALES

BOOK TWO

THE ADVENTURES OF
BRITTANY & LACE

SWEET TALES

BOOK TWO

THE ADVENTURES OF BRITTANY & LACE

LAURIE HYMAN

RED SKY PRESENTS

New York

To my husband Micky, who loves me always,
My darling step-children,
Eric, Scott and Shanna,
and their partners Amy and Joanne

To my loving devoted brothers and sister,
Bert, David, and Nancy
My wonderful sister-in-laws, Ruth and Ellen
Sandy, Susan, and Paulette
My brother-in-law Bernie
and my brother-outlaws Bob, Vaughn and Sam.

A 'Special Thanks' to:

Dorie Riendeau, Lisa Keller, Ellen Saperstein,
Carlo Francesco Pisacane, Robin Veiders,
Leeann Pisacane, Annmarie Gatti,
Belinda Del Pesco, Heather Wood, Jesse Sanchez
Regina Rivera, Anna Felkins
Claudia Woelfle, Barbara Fields, Karin Moore,
and to Marge Tappe for finding our Lace…

And to the South Putnam Animal Hospital
Veterinarians and Staff
and
Dr. Alan Meyers, Animal Clinic of Mt. Vernon
for the great care they have given all our
wonderful felines…

CONTENTS

BRITTANY'S NEW SISTER

CHAPTER ONE

It was a beautiful summer day in the country. The sky was bright blue. Puffy white clouds rolled across Brittany's backyard, protecting the grassy green lawn, plants, gardens, and trees from the heat of the day. Birds flew back and forth from the woods to the bird feeders that hung from apple trees surrounded by pachysandra and long plumed ferns.

"Here we go again," said Britt, a long and lanky tabby cat, to no one in particular. "Off to check out another kitten. So far, so good, for me, they haven't found the right one yet, but this can't last much longer. Love and Man say a new sister is good for me. Humans..."

Brittany, an orange and white ginger queen, was watching and listening to her Mistress. Love, a pretty, petite woman with green eyes and reddish brown hair, was on the phone with a friend. She was pacing back and forth on their covered back porch. These types of conversations had been going on for weeks. Love was in search of a new kitten, a pure white one.

As she chatted away, Brittany heard her say the words 'pet store'. "Really?" replied Love, "You found a white one! Yes, we'll go there right away. My charming man just pulled into the driveway. Thanks. Wait, before you go. How's your puppy Remy? That's great. Yes, let's have happy hour together this weekend." Love hung up the phone and grabbed her purse. She quickly ran down their stone walk to greet her husband and to talk him into taking a ride before lunch.

"Brittany," she called back over her shoulder. "Take care. Your cat door is open. Enjoy the day." Love moved down the steps onto their driveway.

Britt lowered her head and slowly moved towards an open field that bordered the back of their property.

As she passed their woodshed, Nathanial the Woodchuck popped his head out from underneath a pile of wood. The shed had been his home for many years. Nathanial was a revered Elder and Brittany sought him out for advice from time to time.

"Good day to you Britt the Kit," said the woodchuck.

"I'm not a kitten anymore Nathanial. And, I have a weird feeling this isn't going to be such a good day for me, but good day to you."

Nat's nose began to twitch. He dropped the piece of dried wood he was holding and moved out onto the lawn. He raised himself up on two paws and cut Brittany off as she was about to enter the field. "Can you spare a few minutes to chat, Brittany?"

"What's up?"

Nathanial studied the cat for a moment. Britt the Kit had grown into a most impressive cat. She was thin, quick and agile, ran as fast as a rabbit, and loved to climb trees. Her ginger markings were soft, a golden orange mixed with shades of wheat and tan. In addition she had a pure white blaze under her chin and a pure white tip on her long ringed tail. Her eyes, depending on her mood and actions, went from gold to green, sometimes a mixture of both.

"You seem both perturbed and persnickety, Britt. Are your folks off to find you a new kitten, yet again? Have you come to terms with sharing your home with another cat?"

"YES, Nathanial. And NO, I'm not ready for another sister," Brittany whined.

"I understand," said Nathanial. "I know nothing can replace Miss Jade. She was wise, caring, and just, as well as beautiful, charming and fun."

The loss of Miss Jade, Britt's older sister, had hit everyone in the area pretty hard. She was loved and respected, and a great asset among the Elders.

Brittany was now a full grown cat and in her prime. From the time Love and Man had brought her home to their Manhattan apartment as a kitten, Jade had raised, loved, and protected her.

Life was sad without Jade, but Brittany did have Love and Man to herself, and she couldn't deny that she loved the extra affection and attention they needed and wanted to give her. Nathanial had observed the close relationship between

Brittany and her folks and was sensitive to her feelings.

"Britt the Kit, I will reserve the right to call you that on occasion. I understand how you feel, and I know you're in a difficult place right now. But we have a 'situation' and we need you to be part of the solution. That means you must 'suck it up' as the expression goes, and ready yourself to take on a kitten.

"Don't respond!" Nathanial held up a paw. "Just let what I've said settle in your mind and we'll talk about it tomorrow.

"Please meet me here at dawn and we'll discuss this further. When we meet, you can tell me what you found out from Love and Man about the pet store in question. By the way, we are discussing your becoming an Elder, so think about that too."

"Really, I'm old enough to be an Elder? So that makes me not only, not a kitten anymore, but now I'm old too? Wait a minute Nat, how'd you know about the pet store?"

"Brittany, you are not old. You are at the top of your game. All will be clear to you soon. Be on your way." The woodchuck waved her off to the field.

"Thanks, Nathanial. I know I'm a grownup now. See you tomorrow." Brittany walked away with her head hung low.

"Okay," she muttered, "Jade, where are you? I need to be with you..."

A soft voice inside her head answered in a whisper, 'I'm here, always. You know what to do. It's time. Britt.'

"Yeah, you're right. Now I'm supposed to be a cat. I thought it was hard to be a kit, this cat stuff's tough."

Nathanial watched her go and knew she would do what had to be done. What she didn't know was that the situation at the pet store held a special gift for her, a pure white kitten destined to be her sister. Due to unforeseen circumstances and some very bad humans, several animals had been stolen and were in danger. They needed to be rescued immediately and the white kitten was the key.

CHAPTER TWO

Love and her husband, Man, a handsome and gentle man with prematurely white hair, walked into the pet store. As they moved through the store, Love was not pleased with the living conditions of the animals. The store had a sour smell and the creatures looked unhappy.

In the middle of the store, she spotted a glass case that contained kittens. As she moved closer, she noticed that there were four tiny sleeping kittens piled on top of each other. She smiled, amused since they resembled a stack of pancakes with their paws, heads, and tails sticking out.

She softly said, "Hello," and placed her index finger on the head of a white, cocoa, and grey calico kitten. When it opened its eyes, Love's smile vanished. The kitten's round topaz colored eyes were cloudy and crusty with pus around the rims. The little ball of colorful fur rolled off the stack and slowly moved toward her, stumbling a few times, before reaching the edge of the case. Once there, she cried, pleading to be picked up and held.

Hearing the kitten's cries, Man approached and scooped up the tiny animal. "What's the matter?" He held the kitten gently in his strong hands. Turning to his wife he stated, "This kitten is sick and skinny, but adorable."

"I agree. Something is very wrong with this place," Love said and picked up the next kitten from the stack. It was a handsome, grey and white tiger tomcat. She held the kitten up and studied its face and body, then gently squeezed its fur between her fingers. The kitten whimpered and tried to scratch her. Love kissed its head, sighed, and said, "This one is dehydrated, just skin and bones."

At this point the store manager came over, smiling eagerly. "Welcome! These wonderful kittens are on sale. Just for you, I'll give a good price. How about, two kittens for the price of one?"

"That's a great deal," Man replied with a cold look in his dark coffee colored eyes, "but we're just looking for one. We'll call you over if we're interested."

"Okay," said the manager. Just then, a deep growl came from a young male yellow Labrador Retriever in a cage above the man's head. The manager turned and dashed to the back of the store.

Love replaced the tiger kitten she was holding and picked up the next one.

It was grey. Her eyes stung with tears. The kitten's fur reminded her of Jade, the Russian Blue cat she'd loved for eighteen years, who had passed away a few months ago. She put the little feline back in the case.

Love's eyes were immediately drawn to the remaining kitten. She held her breath as she realized the kitten appeared to be pure white." Oh my, what have we here?" She gently lifted the kitten. "Are you the white queen I've been searching for?"

The kitten curled up in her slender hands. Love lifted its chin with her finger and it began to purr. "Open your eyes for me little one." The kitten complied. Her eyes were pastel lime green.

"Look at you! Lovely and so little! You're light as a feather." Love kissed the kitten's head and placed it back in the case. She was becoming emotional.

As soon as Love returned the white kitten to its case, it hissed at her. Turning back, the woman's heart ached. The kitten, now fully awake and alert, tilted her head, questioning where the woman was going. As they studied one another, the young cat's eyes turned a deeper shade of green.

Love knew at that moment that this was her 'Lace'. "Don't worry. I'll be back for you."

Now Love was angry. "This is criminal!" she hissed to her husband, "I thought they were so cute, lying in a pile like that, but now I know it's not cute at all! They're huddled that way to try and stay warm! It's cruel. They're obviously sick and miserable!"

"I think you're right, Love. Let's get out of here. We don't want to bring home any germs to Brittany. Let's go have lunch next door and talk about it."

When the couple left, the kittens quickly huddled together in a tight circle.

"Do you think they'll come back?" asked the white one.

"I think so," said the tiger tomcat. "And I bet they take you out of here. As for the rest of us, who knows?"

"You'll all be fine," barked the yellow Lab pup from his cage on the shelf across from the kittens' case.

"I'm Bert. I'm from the same farm as you. We were all supposed to go to the animal hospital last week when we left the farm, but then the truck stopped for some reason. A bunch of us pups and your litter were taken off and we got moved to another truck and brought here. This place is diseased and filthy. That's why we're all getting sick."

"What does sick mean?" asked the grey kitten. The poor little thing sneezed and fell over.

"It means we need to get rescued quickly or no one will want to give us a proper home. But, I believe those people are going to save us," said the pup with certainty.

By the time they finished their lunch, Love and Man had decided to go to the animal hospital. They agreed they had just witnessed acts of 'animal cruelty' and were now on a mission to save the creatures in the pet store. To accomplish their task, they would need the help of everyone at the animal hospital.

As they left the restaurant and headed to the animal hospital, Love called her lifelong friend Howie and explained the situation. Howie was a lawyer and an animal advocate.

He knew the pet store she was talking about and assured his dear friend he would handle it. He would start by contacting the Chief at the Local SPCA. He promised to help get the pet shop closed and to help with the animal rescue as well.

At the same time, Carlos the Crow, a large black crow with shiny blue-black feathers, landed on the ledge of a roof across the street from the front of the pet store. "Okay, this must be the place Nat was talking about." As he sat perched, he watched Love and Man get into their blue Pathfinder and drive away. 'Brittany's folks,' he thought. 'That could be a good sign. Now, how do I get a look in there?'

As he scanned the area he noticed a child, with a woman, walking on the sidewalk near the store and he caught sight of a large piece of pretzel the boy had just dropped. When the boy bent down to pick it up, the woman yelled at him to "leave it alone!" Without thinking, the large black crow swooped down to get the food and narrowly missed getting hit by a truck that was pulling into the driveway next to the pet store.

Carlos cawed at the truck, picked up the pretzel with his claws, and followed the vehicle into the parking lot, where it stopped at the back entrance of the pet store.

"Ah ha," cawed the crow. What he saw made sense. The truck parked and the driver got out and opened the back door. He unloaded a crate of kittens and entered the back door of the store. The crow dropped the pretzel and flew to the back of the truck. He peered in and asked the animals inside, "What's going on here?"

"My Mom," said a black poodle puppy, "told me I was going to the Vets, and then to my new home with a nice family. What's this place?"

"Okay kid, stay calm, help is on the way." Carlos answered. He took flight and headed to the animal hospital. "This is crazy! No one gets away with stealing babies around here." He flew away, flapping his wings, and cawing his head off because he was very angry.

CHAPTER THREE

Carlos the Crow circled the strip mall that housed the pet store. As he gained altitude he flew over a boat marina on a large lake. He spotted speed boats with tow-lines pulling people on water skis. The skiers swooshed and slid over the sparkling water, dodging teenagers on jet skis, and others in row boats. There were beaches where people could lay in the sun and swim, and private homes and restaurants close to the lake.

The crow then flew higher into the blue sky, circling over the lake community, which included local shops and stores, homes and yards, houses of worship, and schools with large green sports fields. Finally, he followed the road that would take him directly to the animal hospital.

When Carlos reached his destination, he once again circled high in the sky to check out the area surrounding the animal hospital. He spotted Love and Man heading into the large red brick building.

"Good," he cawed. "Wow, when Nat decides to take

care of a problem he doesn't waste any time. I wonder how he got them involved. Whatever, I have to find that Vet Cat, and make sure he's doing his part. What a mess."

"Oy, what is it Miss Jade always said? Oh yeah, she would hope this tale has a happy ending... Wonderful queen, I miss her.

"Jade's sister, Brittany, has grown up to be very nice. We're lucky she's fond of crows. That cat can move fast as a rabbit. At times all we'd see of her was a flash of orange!"

...'I remember when Britt the Kit was just a kitten, and there were three of us eating bread under their birdfeeder. That little kitten snuck right up behind us. She was quiet and quick. We didn't hear her. It's a good thing for us, that my Missus Erma was keeping lookout for us in a tree. She thought it was funny, so she waited until Britt was about to attack us. Then she silently swooped down at the last minute and spread her impressive black wings gently around the kitten's back. It was the funniest thing to watch. Britt the Kit flew three feet in the air! It seemed like she got to her cat door without her paws ever touching the ground...'

As Carlos descended to the animal hospital building, he spotted Toezer the Vet Cat at the back entrance, sunning himself.

Toezer was a large calico tomcat. His fur was white for

the most part, with brown tabby markings on the top of his head and ears and above his eyes. The tabby pattern also appeared to drip down his back and along the sides of his body to resemble an English riding saddle. His extra bushy, tabby ringtail completed the picture. He was interesting to look at and quite handsome.

"Hey Toez," cawed the crow, "how's it going?" he landed about six feet away from the cat.

"Hi Carlos, what brings you over here today?"

"You!"

"What's up?" The large cat sat up, knowing it must be important if Carlos, an Elder, had showed up to meet with him.

"There's a scam going on at the pet store in town. Men are stealing and selling pups and kits. Can you believe it? Stupid humans!" The large black bird hopped around and flapped his wings.

"Listen, two nice humans just went inside the Vet's office. They belong to Britt the Kit. You know her, yes?"

Toezer nodded in reply.

"Good, they just came from the pet store in question. Go see what's happening and come back and tell me. I'll wait. Okay?" The crow lowered his head and stared at the cat with one beady, steel grey eye, waiting for the cat's response.

"Of course, I won't be long," replied Toezer, as he entered the open back door.

Once inside the cat was free to move about. As a Vet Cat, Toezer was very unique and astute. He acted as a 'go-between' for the animals, explaining to them what was going on, and keeping them as calm as possible. He assisted the staff when necessary, and interacted with the pets' owners only on rare occasions.

He searched for Love and Man and found them with two veterinarians. Toezer listened for a few minutes and dashed back outside.

"It's all good, Carlos. The humans are on it. I knew there was a problem last week when a group of animals arrived from Anna's farm. They were half crazed because a litter of kittens and a bunch of pups had been taken off the truck when it stopped for gas. It took days to calm them down. Are the missing pups and kittens okay? Is that what you're trying to find out about?"

"Yes it is. Why didn't you tell anyone?" asked the crow with flapping wings.

"I did! Calm yourself. I'm the one who reported the problem in the first place! I sent word to the farm and I reported it to Nathanial."

"Good work, Toez," the crow was a bit embarrassed. "Nobody tells me anything. They say 'Carlos do this, do that.' So now I know why Nat has me flying all over the place. Anyway, good, I'll tell him the latest news. Thanks." Carlos flew away without another word.

Toezer just shook his head and went back inside. He wanted to reassure the other youngsters at the Vets that their families and friends were going to get the help they needed.

When Love and Man got home and opened their back

porch door, Brittany was waiting patiently on one of the kitchen counter tops.

Love moved to her quickly, kissed the top of her head, and scooped the cat up into her arms. "What a day we had Brittany!" Brittany didn't like to be held this way, but she adored Love and stayed still for as long as she could bear it. "Oh, my sweet kit," Love mused, placing the cat on the floor. "Just holding you calms me down. Thanks."

Love gave the cat fresh cold water and went over what had transpired since they'd left that morning. "Brittany, you can't image how sick these kittens are. The other animals at the pet store didn't look well either, but we're going to fix all of that.

"Jennifer at the animal hospital took care of everything. Howie will oversee all the plans. The Local SPCA will be called. The pet store will be closed, the animals will be taken to the Vets to be checked out, and then they will be temporarily returned to Anna's farm. From there, homes will be found for everyone.

"Britt, come here please," she bent down and crooked her finger to call the cat closer to her, "I think, and I hope you're ready. There is a white kitten among the animals. If she's not too sick, I'd like to bring her home. She'll be your new sister. You'll be the big sister now, like Jade was to you. You'll raise her, and watch over her, until she's grown. Is that okay with you?"

Brittany, couldn't help herself, she meowed 'NO' and ran out of the house.

Frustrated and angry, Britt ran across her land and into the woods, jumping over rocks and under tree limbs, meowing and hissing, grumbling to herself. She didn't stop until she was deep in the woods that bordered their property.

"Hey Kit, I know just how you feel, been there done that. Wanna talk about it?" said a voice high in a tree.

"No. Leave me alone, Sky. Nat says I have to suck it up! Whatever, that means. It hurts! My life is changing and I have no control over it. None! I don't want to raise a kitten. I understand the part about Jade, but they can't just bring home another cat and call it my sister."

Sky, a handsome black and white tiger tomcat, jumped out of the tree and sat near Brittany. "How about you just think of it as a kitten that's helpless, and you're willing to help it through a tough time. Human labels are strange, but somehow those labels give them comfort. You don't have to call the kitten 'sister'. Just help out. You're good at that. I've seen you. You saved my life, remember?"

"Yeah, but that was different. You only stayed with us for a couple of weeks and then you went back to the farm."

"So take in this little one, and help it. Let's say for one turning of the moon? Would that work for you?" Sky rubbed against the smaller ginger cat.

"No! That's not true! I can't keep it for just a month. I'll have to live with it for the rest of my life. Thanks Sky, for trying to help, but..."

"But what? You're being selfish Brittany. That's not like you."

"Yes it is. I was always 'the brat'. When I was younger, I asked so many questions and no one wanted to or had the time to answer me. I'd do just about anything to get someone to play with me. It was okay, I guess. Eventually I got attention one way or another. Now that I'm grown up, I can see that."

"It's that way for all youngsters, Britt. Me included. Look at all the trouble I used to get into. I never listened."

"Yeah, you were bad, but fun. How's life at the farm? I haven't been over there this summer?"

In the distance, the sound of a dog barking reached the cats and interrupted their conversation. Their ears perked up and they listened. Sky touched his nose to Brittany's. The handsome black and white tiger's deep blue eyes softened. He was sympathetic to her situation.

"I gotta go. Think about it, Britt. Help out. You won't be sorry, I promise."

"Easy for you to say," Britt rubbed against the younger cat. "Thanks Sky, I promise I'll think about it. Be safe."

"Bye," said Sky, as he took off, following the sound of the barking dog.

Sky quickly traveled through the woods, ran across a big field, jumped over a couple of streams, and crossed several roads. When he finally reached the barking dog, he stopped short in front of Henry, the stately, black coated, male Labrador Retriever. Henry was an Elder and both he and Sky lived on Anna's farm.

"Sky, how did it go with Brittany?" asked Henry.

"Not sure Henry. Brittany's pretty stubborn."

"Did you tell her that the pet store kittens were your kittens?"

"No, you told me not to, remember? You said she had to come to a decision on her own for things to work out. Right?"

"Yes. That is what I said. It will be better, going forward, if she decides to accept the white kitten and moves ahead with her life without Miss Jade.

"From what I understand, your kittens are very ill. They've been removed from the pet store and are now at the animal hospital. We don't know how long they'll be kept there, or how strong they'll be once they leave the Vets. And, we don't know whether they'll ever be well enough to come back to the farm or go to new homes.

"Their fate, as yet, is undecided. You do know Brittany wouldn't hesitate to take your white kitten if she knew it was yours, right?"

"Yesss." hissed Sky. "I wouldn't force Brittany to do anything, even though I know she would. Henry, please don't think for a minute my litter won't survive. I won't rest until they're all safe and settled. I know how scared they must be, and sick, and tired, and hungry. I'm their Dad and I won't let them down." The tiger tom now growled at Henry, "My kittens will live! Got it?"

"Yes Sky, I believe you. Please know that plans have been put in place to save all the animals that were in that rotten place. Toezer will let us know their condition tonight. I will come and find you."

"No!" Sky's fur puffed out from the top of his head to the tip of his tail. I'll find you! I'm headed there now, and I'll let you know what I find out."

"Sky, you do know I have kin in this fight, too. One of the pups at that pet store is my grandson, Bert."

"No I didn't. I'll ask Toezer about him for you."

Henry cocked his head and looked at the determined tiger cat. "You've grown up to be a fine substantial tom, Sky. And your eyes still tell your story as they did when you were a kitten. Right now they are fierce, crystal clear, and true blue. Be on your way. You are officially assigned the mission of letting us all know how the rescue went. You will report directly to me on all of the animals from our farm."

"I'll be back by sunset, and thanks Henry, for believing in me. It means a lot coming from you."

As Sky made his way to the animal hospital, he had a lot on his mind. Brittany had literally saved his life when he was just a kitten. He'd lived with her, Jade, and their folks, Love and Man, for weeks after having been seriously attacked and injured by a nasty bully cat. He still had a scar on his neck from the incident.

Britt's sister, Jade, had kept her word over the years and taught Sky how to grow strong, both physically and mentally. Now he was a grown tomcat, with his first litter of kittens, and all four of them were in trouble. Because of what Sky had learned from Jade and Brittany, he was up to the challenge of helping his kittens.

He knew that 'Snow', his name for the pure white kitten, would somehow wind up with Brittany, but he wasn't told the details. He also knew that his son Scamp, a grey and white tiger tom, and his two young queens, Willa the grey, and Coco, the white, grey, and cocoa calico, would all need good homes. Sky knew it was up to him to make sure they were taken care of.

When Sky reached the brick building that held his litter, he stopped short. The few times he'd been there, he'd always been carried in by humans. He sat down in the middle of the parking lot and meowed in frustration. "How am I going to get inside? What was I thinking?"

"Calm yourself Sky." Toezer the Vet Cat called from the top step of the stairs that led to the front entrance of the building. "Here about your kittens, are you?"

"Yes Sir, I am. Please tell me. Are they all okay?" asked the worried Dad.

"They will all survive. Come with me, now. I will take you to them. But, you must agree to do exactly as I say. The humans can't know we are actually intelligent and take care of our own. Yes?"

"Sure Toezer, anything you want from me, you got it." By now Sky was nose to nose with the equally large, white and brown calico tomcat. "Lead the way, and thanks. I gotta see them for myself. Oh, Henry asked me to report back to him on the condition of his grandson Bert, the yellow lab pup, and the others that were rescued. You'll fill me in before I leave, right?"

"Yes, Sky," he purred, thinking what a pleasure it was to interact with this pleasant tom instead of that cocky crow. But all in all, he thought to himself, having all this company from the outside area was kinda nice. It was a nice distraction from his usual routine. He spent most of his time with frightened or sick animals and their humans, or the busy doctors and equally busy staff.

"By the way" he told Sky, "Bert, as you call him, is quite the pup. Even at this young age, he's taken on the role of 'leader' of his rescued group."

Toezer led Sky into the animal hospital through his cat door by the main entrance. The cleaning staff was due to arrive in about an hour. Toezer explained to Sky that he would have to leave by the time the crew arrived.

Sky was skittish. He wasn't used to such an enclosed space or the smells and sounds that surrounded him, but he was very determined to see his litter. His kittens needed to know their father hadn't deserted them.

"Sky, chill out, please," said Toezer, aware of his discomfort. "This is my domain and I excel at taking care of everyone, humans and animals alike!"

"Okay, sorry. So where are they?"

"In the room down the hall, the one without a door, so we can enter easily."

The two cats entered the large room. The walls were lined with cages stacked one on top of the other. Each stack had four cages. Dogs with larger cages were on the bottom, cats with smaller cages were on the top. The pet store rescue situation had made the room unusually crowded.

Sky began to meow, calling to his litter. Toezer shushed him, "Quiet Sky, don't wake everyone up. I'd just gotten them settled when I heard you screaming in the parking lot. Come with me and be quiet, please!"

"Okay," Sky replied and sighed. This visit and assignment was tougher than he thought it would be.

Now that Sky had calmed down, Toezer explained his litter's situation. "Your kittens are strong. They were given a thorough exam by the Vets. Their temperatures were taken, and those with a fever were given shots of antibiotics. They've been bathed to remove any ticks and fleas, and they've been de-wormed. Everyone was hydrated and fed with special hospital food."

"Really, they needed all that! I've gotta see them now. Where are they?"

"Over here. I moved Bert into their cage for extra warmth." Toezer jumped onto an exam table across from the kitten's cage and motioned to Sky to join him.

The Vet Cat pointed to a 'Do Not Disturb' sign, placed on the kittens' cage for the cleaning crew. "That sign insures they won't be touched until morning."

Sky couldn't believe what he saw. His kittens were curled all over the young yellow Lab pup. They were under his chin, along his back and two were under his front paws snuggled next to his belly. "Wow, Bert sure is a good guy!"

"Yes he is," said Toezer. "Do you really need to wake

them? They seem to be sleeping peacefully."

"I don't know," Sky was torn. He wanted his litter to know he was there, but he didn't want to wake them and rile them up. He knew they'd want to see him, but now he understood that they certainly needed their rest.

"What should I do, Toez? You know best."

Bert opened his eyes, aware that he was being watched. When he saw Sky, he sighed and closed his eyes again.

"I think," said Toezer, "you just got your answer." Toezer placed his paw on Sky's back, "Best to let them be for now. I will tell them you were here and you are welcome to come back at the same time tomorrow, if they're still here. Will that work for you?"

"Yeah, I think so. They must have had one heck of a day. Please tell them I said everything's gonna be alright."

"Yes, and it will. Let's get you out of here. Be on your way, so you can let their mother and Henry know all is well. And, please tell Henry I said he has one amazing grandson in Bert."

"I will and thanks. You are really good at your job, Toezer. I feel better too!"

CHAPTER FOUR

Nathanial paced in front of the woodshed. It had been his and his family's home for many moons. He had lived there long before Love and Man moved in and was quite content to have them as neighbors. They had a high regard for all the animals and for the land that was their home, as well as the surrounding area.

Deep in thought, he hadn't heard the snap of Brittany's cat door open and close, and he didn't realize the cat was sitting a few feet away from him. The first he knew of her arrival was the sound of her rich purr. He turned and observed the beautiful queen, patiently sitting and waiting for him to notice her.

"Morning, Britt." Nathanial eyed her carefully. She looked radiant and strong, and her golden fur glistened in the early morning sunlight.

"Good morning to you, too, Nathanial. I think it's a good one, because you'll be happy with me. I'm ready to 'step up' as you asked yesterday. I've learned 'Lace' is my new sister's name. My folks are very concerned about her, as you thought they would be. Can you believe she's the size of a young chipmunk? She will definitely need help and I will help her, promise."

"Britt, you've warmed my heart with satisfaction. Well done…" As a tear ran down Nat's face, he clapped his paws together in happiness and relief.

"Take it easy Nat. I didn't realize you were this stressed out. It'll be okay."

"Yes, we'll all be okay, as you say. I couldn't tell you before because, well, you had to decide on your own, but 'Lace' as you call her is part of Sky's first litter. She's one of four. And, Sky too will be pleased and relieved with your decision."

"Sky's daughter? Wow! Why didn't you tell me? I wouldn't have had to think about it at all, if either one of you had just told me!"

"We knew that, which is why we held our tongues. Even though we knew that destiny would bring the white kitten to you, you had to come to accept her on your own, freely, and for the right reasons. You had to choose for yourself, Britt. Understand?"

"Yeah, I think I do. Thanks. Will I ever be as wise as you?"

The woodchuck tilted his head and studied the cat, "Yes Brittany, in time. Please let me know when your 'Lace' arrives so we may have a proper and joyous greeting."

"Sure Nat, and thanks for being my Elder. You've taken the time to teach me a lot over the years and I'm thankful for your friendship, wisdom, and most of all, your putting up with me."

"You're a pleasure, Britt. We're all grateful to have you among us. Peace..."

The two animals went their separate ways.

Brittany was indeed at peace with her decision and her acceptance of Lace, the tiny white kitten that would be home soon.

At the animal hospital, the kittens and Bert were also at peace. They slept through the night, as did the rest of the animals from the pet store. At dawn, Jennifer, a soft spoken lady, arrived for work at the animal hospital.

Her first job was to check on the animals. When she entered the room that held Bert and the kittens, she noticed immediately that Bert's cage was empty, but quickly found him in the kitten's cage. She looked around and spotted Toezer meekly sitting in the corner of the room.

Jennifer smiled, went over to Toezer, and gave his head a pat. "So, this is your doing? Okay, I understand. Actually it was a good idea. This way the kittens felt safe and protected."

The kittens and pup woke to the squeak of their cage door being opened. Jennifer placed a large bowl inside the cage.

"Morning, come have some fresh cold water," she called.

The kittens scampered off Bert and headed for the bowl.

Bert stood up, yawned, stretched, and looked up questioningly at the woman with his big brown eyes. She smiled and gently pulled on the flea collar that had been placed around his neck after his bath the day before.

"Come with me, please." Bert let out a soft woof and complied, as she led him out of his cage and onto the floor where water and dog food were waiting for him. He devoured the food and took a long drink of water.

In the meantime, Jennifer fed the kittens. They were very hungry and ate up the delicious healthy food. She then slipped a bright blue, long collared leash around the young pup's neck and led him out the back door.

The kittens went crazy. They meowed and cried, panicked because their protector had been taken from them.

"Where did Bert go?" yelled the grey and white tiger tom.

"I do not know," replied the calico.

The white kitten then looked out the window and could see Bert with the woman. "It's okay, he's taking a poop."

"Why didn't he go in the litter box like us?" asked the grey kitten.

"Because," answered the grey tiger, "dogs around here get walked. They don't have litter boxes like us. They're too big."

Satisfied that Bert was still close by, the felines took turns in the litter box in the corner of the cage, and then bathed themselves and each other.

When Bert returned with the nice lady, he was placed in a separate cage next to the kittens. Jennifer realized life would be quieter if the kittens were near their yellow Lab friend. She then attended to the next cage of the animals.

"Everyone okay this morning?" Bert barked, addressing the four kittens.

"Yeah, we're all good Bert, thanks for letting us sleep with you last night. You're really warm and soft," said Willa the grey kitten.

"My pleasure, your purring comforted me last night, so, a 'thanks' to you too, is in order. By the way, your Dad came by last night. He wanted you all to know that everything is going to be okay and that he'd see you soon.

"I also ran into Toezer outside. He told me to let you all know that some of us are moving out later today, so be prepared. Just be strong and have faith that the best arrangements have been made for everyone. Our Earth Mother and the people here either found us good homes or we will be returned to Anna's farm. Got it?"

The kittens got very quiet and snuggled next to one another without responding to Bert, which he understood. He had a home with Henry on the farm, but he knew their future was still uncertain and scary. "Alright then, we'll see what the day brings."

By the end of the day, Bert and all of the animals were gone from the hospital room except for the little white queen. She never thought she could feel so alone. Being sick was nothing compared to being all alone!

Just then, Toezer appeared. "Had a bad day little one?" he asked. He climbed to the kitten's cage, opened the latch with his nail, and climbed in. "Come here to me," he motioned with his paw. The young cat weighed just over a pound, but stood her ground and hissed hot and fierce at the older cat.

"Now, now" said the Vet Cat. "You're not the first animal to be the last to go."

The kitten sat down, her round green eyes softening as she looked up into the Vet Cat's caring tortoiseshell colored eyes, searchingly and pleadingly.

Toezer thought, 'she's breaking my heart'. Soothingly he said, "You'll be going to your destined home tonight. You will have a good life. Now, come here to me." The kitten ran to the cat and jumped onto his face and started licking him. She began to purr, the deepest, sweetest purr Toezer had ever heard.

"Thank you, I didn't know being alive could be so very hard, Toezy."

"I know. Trust that all will be as it should be soon. Everyone has been working very hard to make sure you wind up where you're supposed to be. Why don't you settle down with me and I'll stay here until you're picked up. You can tell me your story about life on the farm and what happened after you left. Okay?"

"Okey Dokey, I'll tell you." The cat and the kitten cuddled together…

"Life on the farm was fun. A lot of us lived there," Lace began, "My Mama and Papa were wonderful to my litter, except Papa had this thing about us leaving the barn. He'd freak out whenever we tried to sneak out. Anna, our Mistress, was also wonderful. She played with us and we liked to make her giggle. It's a neat sound."

"That it is. One of the nicer sounds humans make. Have you noticed that their eyes sparkle when they giggle?"

"Yes I have! Anyway, Anna really liked Bert. I saw tears in her eyes when he was loaded onto the truck. We were already inside. It made me sad for her. Did he go back to the farm? Will she see him again?"

"Yes, Bert returned to the farm this afternoon with the rest of your litter."

"Are they going to stay there? I'm gonna miss them so much."

"What I do know is they will all remain in the area, either at the farm or in new homes. So you should be close enough to visit. Your Papa insisted on that, and one of the Elders, Nathanial the Woodchuck, took care of the arrangements. I'm sure you'll see them all soon."

"Thanks Toezy, you can call me Snow. That's what my Papa calls me."

"Do you know about the naming of cats?" asked Toezer.

"You mean that we have three names?" answered Lace.

"Yes." Toezer usually avoided this issue with kittens coming through the hospital, but in this particular situation, he felt he needed to say something.

"Snow is one of your names. When you leave here you will be receiving your 'everyday' name from your new Mistress. That will be the name I'll know you by. Understand?"

"Not really? I like the name 'Snow'. I've never seen snow. My Mama says it's beautiful, but very cold."

Toezer sighed. Kittens could drive one crazy with their curiosity and questions. It was not his place to take this particular conversation any further. "Yes, your Mama is correct."

"She also said it melts. I don't want to melt!"

The Vet Cat said no more. His ears perked up when he heard the sounds of people entering the building. Toezer could tell by their movement that they were heading into the waiting area. The kitten heard it, too.

"It's time. I need to get out of here. You should use the litter box and bathe. I'm happy for you."

"Will I ever see you again Toezy? I like you very much."

"Yes, of course. Next month you'll be back for a checkup. I will see you then. I gotta go now. I have a feeling you'll grow to be a very special cat. Have a wonderful life!" Toezer patted the kitten on the head and exited the cage.

Toezer was relieved to be on his way. He hurried to greet whoever had arrived. It was part of his job. Hopefully, his last charge of the day would be on her way home.

The kitten did as Toezer suggested and quickly groomed herself. She then lowered her head in a whispered prayer... "Please, Earth Mother, let me be done with this sick, bad, lonely stuff. Please let this next part of my tale have a good new beginning. Pleeease let me be safe and loved."

CHAPTER FIVE

It was early the next morning and bright sunlight was slipping into the master bedroom through the slats in the wooden window shades. Brittany sat at the end of the big bed quietly watching Love and Man sleeping. Their new white kitten was nestled between them, also sound asleep. Love had found the white feline she was looking for, and they had named her Lace. 'I guess,' Britt thought to herself, 'I should let them sleep,' so she snuggled next to Love, and closed her eyes.

It had been a tough night for the tiny white kitten. At first, when Love and Man brought her home from the animal hospital, she was placed in a separate room with the door closed, away from Brittany, as is the custom when a pet is introduced into a new home.

Lace was still on antibiotic medicine because she had an infection and had been running a fever. During the night, Britt heard her crying, but couldn't get into the room. The kitten's cries relayed to Britt that she was in pain and scared. The older cat meowed, "Stay calm Lace, I'll get you help." Lace whimpered, curled up on the soft bed Love had made for her and waited.

Brittany ran down the hall to Love and Man's bedroom and jumped onto the big bed. They were sleeping peacefully. The cat began to purr and waited for a few moments. 'I don't want to wake them, but Lace is definitely in trouble,' she thought to herself.

Love opened her eyes when she heard Britt's purring. With her arm she motioned for the cat to come closer. When Britt didn't move, Love sat up. "What's up Britt?" she whispered.

Brittany jumped off the bed and let out a loud meow. Love immediately shushed her and got out of bed whispering, "Quiet Britt, don't wake him," referring to her husband, who remained sound asleep.

"What is it? Is something wrong with Lace?" Britt meowed softly and took off down the hall towards the closed door where the kitten was staying. Love jumped out of bed and followed the white tip of Brittany's tail.

As soon as the woman opened the porch door, Britt ran into the room and then slowly approached the kitten. "It's gonna be okay Lace. Love will help you. I'm Brittany, your new housemate. Britt then gave the kitten a few sniffs. The way Lace smelled confirmed she was indeed in trouble. Britt leaned down to touch the kitten's nose and purred reassuringly. Lace lifted her head and they touched noses.

This was their first greeting. "It's nice to meet you, too. Thanks for helping me, Brittany."

"That's what I'm here for Lace, now and always."

"Brittany, please move away," Love whispered. The ginger cat did as she was asked. She jumped up onto a card table and sat quietly. Love moved to her kitten and touched the top of her head. "You're burning up!" She lifted the kitten into her arms. Lace anxiously looked up at her new Mistress.

Love let out a deep sigh, "I will take care of you. I promise. You're going to get through this and have a good healthy life with us."

Love left the room with the kitten tucked under her arm and headed for the kitchen. She placed Lace on the counter and searched through the papers that Jennifer had given her when they left the animal hospital. When she found what she was looking for, she reached for the phone.

"Be still. I'm going to call for help." The worried woman picked up the phone and punched in the number for a 24/7 Emergency Animal Hotline. She tapped her long finger nails, impatiently waiting while the phone rang.

A gentle, young male voice finally answered. "How can we help you this morning?" Love glanced at the kitchen clock. It was three o'clock in the morning.

"Hi," said Love. "I hope you can help me over the phone. I have a very sick two-month-old kitten. We brought her home from the animal hospital tonight. She's on antibiotics, but she's burning up with a fever and I don't know what to do. Can you help me, please?"

"Hold on for a doctor, please," said the young man.

Love noticed the kitten was shivering, so she picked her up and held her close to keep her warm. Brittany, in the meantime, had jumped onto a pass-through ledge that separated the kitchen and living room.

"Hi, this is Doctor Meyers, what seems to be the emergency?" Love and the doctor spoke for about fifteen minutes. She gave the doctor a quick rundown of what had happened to Lace and her litter, about how they'd gone from the farm to the pet store, and then to the animal hospital. She ended with bringing Lace home, and what had happened within the last few hours.

"Sounds like you all had a long day. I don't think there is anything to worry about tonight. Give Lace another dose of antibiotics. Keep her close to you, so you can reassure her that all is well, and try to get some rest. The kitten has been through a lot in the last couple of weeks."

Doctor Meyers then continued. "Besides being sick, she's probably having some nightmares, which could be the reason her fever spiked. She'll need some time to settle down and heal.

"The fact that your other cat came to get you when she realized the kitten was in distress is a good sign. Keep her close as well, so the kitten knows she's nearby. If Lace is still feverish in the morning, call your Vet. Please feel free to call back. We're here for Lace and her family."

"Thanks," Love said, and hung up the phone.

Holding Lace, Love turned to Brittany. "Okay Britt, you were right to get me up. But, now you're going to have to help me, and I know you won't like it.

"You've been great so far with accepting a new kitten into the house. I didn't expect you to have to share the rest of your home with your sister this soon. Especially not our bed, but, I have to give Lace more medicine and take her back to bed with us, Doctor's orders." Love waited for her cat's reaction.

Brittany let out a deep growl. She understood Love's intentions. Lace jumped out of Love's arms and fell on the floor. Love picked her up and set her back down on a kitchen counter away from Brittany.

"And," Love said, picking up a prickly Brittany, "you're coming to bed, too. Lace will feel safer if you're there. She's not used to us yet. Okay?"

Britt understood and collapsed into Love's arms, surrendering. She couldn't be upset. She knew their kitten needed help. She'd made a promise, and would keep her word, even though she didn't like it one bit.

Lace watched the woman and her cat interact. 'Wow,' she thought, 'they're amazing with each other. I hope Brittany can accept me. I think I could be really happy here.'

When Love, Britt, and Lace slipped quietly into bed, Love placed the kitten on a pillow between her and her husband. Brittany moved to her normal sleeping place next to Love on the other side. She always slept there so she could get on and off the bed easily, without waking her

Mistress during the night.

Love settled into bed facing the kitten. She placed one of her slender hands next to Lace's back. Brittany snuggled into the small of Love's back. They were all asleep within minutes.

A few hours later, Man yawned, stretched, and sat up in bed. He smiled at the sight of his wife flanked by their two cats and wondered what had gone on during the night. He quietly left the bed, trying not to wake anyone. Brittany felt his movement. She opened her eyes and lifted her head. Man signaled to her 'to come' with a wave of his arm. The cat jumped quickly off the bed and followed him into the kitchen. She knew he would give her breakfast and let her outside.

Man put on a pot of coffee, fed Britt, and put her collar on. He then grabbed a container of bird food and a few slices of bread, and headed out to feed the birds, squirrels, and chipmunks. As soon as he opened the door, the cat ran out.

Brittany heard Carlos' caw and headed to the woods on their property.

"Caw Caw Caw," yelled the large black crow. "Brittany, what's going on? How's the kitten? Everyone wants to know. I've been waiting for you!"

"Yeah, I figured that. It was a long night. She's still pretty sick, but she'll be okay, I think. She slept with us. She's still asleep in our bed with Love."

"But, of course, she slept with you. Who else would she sleep with? We crows always sleep together. Doesn't everyone?"

"I don't know," said Britt. "I guess you could be right."

"So I can let everyone know… What's her name? I heard she had a few… "

"My folks have named her Lace. I felt bad for her last night Carlos, so I guess that means I care about her, right?"

"Sure." The crow swooped down from the tree branch he was sitting on and landed next to Brittany. "It's a good thing, Britt, having this other cat to live with, not just your humans. You'll see." Carlos extended his large black wing and patted the cat's back.

"So off I go now. They have me going all over the place, from here to the farm, then back to the animal hospital where I started out this morning. Toezer was so hissy," griped the crow. "He wouldn't even let me finish my breakfast. He opened his claws and swatted at me to get over here and find you. I'm not a messenger pigeon – I'm a crow!"

"It seems like Lace gets into everyone's hearts pretty quick." Brittany found Carlos most amusing. She knew that despite his complaints, he loved being an Elder and doing his part to help animals in trouble. "Yeah, I understand, but you do have wings to fly around quickly and go directly from place to place."

"Ha!" said Carlos, "It's funny you should say that. We crows are known for the old saying 'as the crow flies', which is just what you said, Britt the Kit."

"That's cool, Carlos. Do you want me to save you a trip and tell Nathanial that Lace is okay?"

"Thanks! Good idea. I couldn't find him when I got

here," said Carlos as he began his ascent into the trees. Brittany watched as the large black bird began to flap his wings, then leave the ground, and fly straight into the air until he cleared the woods. The crow headed north, as the crow flies, back towards the animal hospital, to give Toezer the good news.

Brittany stayed where she was, alone for a moment, and thought, 'I'm lucky I have these older friends around me. They're not only teaching me, but they're helping me get through this big change. Yeah, I think it's gonna be all right. I'd better report to Nat and then check on Lace.'

Love heard the kitchen door open and close. "It must be morning," she said as she looked over at the adorable white kitten sleeping on the pillow right next to her head. Their noses were only inches apart. Lace began to purr before she was fully awake, her eyes were still closed. 'Good,' thought Love, 'hopefully it means she's feeling better.'

The woman stayed perfectly still and watched as her beautiful new kitten came to life. First, Lace's front paws pushed out against Love's arm, then came the beginning of a big yawn. When Lace was finished and her mouth closed, she realized with surprise and delight that she was safe and warm, and that she didn't feel sick any more.

As Love studied the kitten, she admired her white fur and smiled at her delicate pink nose and mouth. She also noticed a hint of pink within her ears. When Lace's eyes popped open, Love held her breath and a single tear slipped from her eyes. Her kitten's eyes were jade green.

Spotting the tear falling down the nice lady's face, Lace moved closer and licked the tear away with her pink tongue. She then placed her soft pink paw pad on Love's cheek. They stayed that way for a moment until Brittany pounced on the bed.

As Britt watched the apparent intimacy between Love and Lace, waves of jealousy filled her body. She couldn't help herself and hissed.

Luckily Man entered the bedroom and scooped her up into his strong loving arms. "It's okay Britt, you'll always be our kit," and kissed her head. "Come with me and I'll give you a treat." Love and Man exchanged a knowing smile as he carried Britt out of the room. Brittany and Lace had just begun their 'getting to know you' stage.

Once again Love and Lace were alone. Love picked up the kitten and placed her on her chest. "Brittany will be fine. You'll just need to be patient with her."

Lace purred and nuzzled into her neck. Love smiled and wrapped Lace lovingly in her arms.

The kitten's fever was gone, her head and ears were cool, and her perfect pink nose was wet and cold. 'Lace is home and healing,' thought Love, 'and I am too.'

CHAPTER SIX

Brittany and Lace were in the living room of their country home. Like many sisters, they'd hit a few bumps in the road, but were now truly attached to one another. Britt was pretty content with her kitten and Lace adored and looked up to her big sister.

The cats were sitting, side by side, next to their cat carriers. When Lace sniffed one of the two, she picked up her own scent and realized she had been in that carrier on the night Love and Man brought her home.

Now she was scared! "Brittany, where am I going?" She cried. "Please don't let them take me away! I'll be good and stay out of the big bed, if that's what you want."

"Chill out kit," Britt was amused. "You're here to stay Lace. Love and Man are just taking you back to the animal hospital for your one month check-up. So, calm down and be still. Be good or Love will get upset. Okay?"

Britt gave the kitten's head a gentle smack and shooed

her into her cat carrier. "Get used to it, Lace. I told you we live in two places, the country and the city. This is how we travel with Love and Man. We go back and forth in these carriers in our Pathfinder."

"Really? I still don't understand how we can live someplace else, when we already live here." Lace was confused, but she'd learned over the last few weeks that Brittany was always truthful with her, even when she didn't like or understand what she had to say. "Never mind, Brittany. Will I see Toezer at the Vets?"

"Yeah, I'm sure he'll want to see you. If you look around the parking lot as they wheel you in, you'll see someone else, too. Remember, be good and don't hurt anyone. Got it?"

"Okey Dokey, I got it." Lace settled and sat in the carrier. Love came into the room, approached the carrier, zipped the kitten in, and pulled up a long handle. The carrier had four wheels. As Lace was rolled away from Brittany she firmly planted her paws on the soft mat. When they were leaving the house, Lace dug her claws into the mat for leverage. Lace meowed to Britt, "This is kinda fun. I'll be good."

Britt watched from the kitchen window until their Pathfinder pulled out of the driveway. "Okay, the house is quiet and I have it all to myself. Thanks, Earth Mother, it's been a while. I think a peaceful cat nap is in my future." Britt found a sunny warm spot on a soft chair and began to bathe. When she was done she circled several times, curled up, and started to drift off. "What a month," she sighed and fell asleep.

Love took Lace out of her carrier once the car doors were closed. "You can sit with me, little one," she said and placed the kitten on her lap between her hands.

"It will be fine, Love. Please don't worry," said Man, as he drove them to the animal hospital. "Lace is healthy. She just needs to be cleared by her doctor and start getting her vaccinations. Okay?"

"Yes, you're right. I'm fine," his wife replied.

But Lace knew better. Love seemed anxious. Lace began to purr, because that always seemed to calm Love down. The kitten had come to adore these two humans and enjoyed pleasing them.

The Pathfinder pulled into the parking lot of the animal hospital. Man parked under a tree to shade the SUV from the summer sun. Love put Lace back in her carrier, placed her on the ground and rolled her towards the entrance.

The little white kitten looked out through the mesh flap on her carrier. She began to search for whomever Brittany told her she might see. It only took a moment for her to spot the black and white, handsome tiger tomcat, with piercing blue eyes. She was about to cry out but stopped herself before she made a sound.

Instead, she locked eyes and sent good positive thoughts to her Papa, who in turn sighed and warmed at the sight of his kitten. Sky headed towards Love and Man meowing 'hello.' The two humans stopped and bent down to say hello to their old friend.

"Sky! What are you doing here?" questioned Man. "I

hope you're not sick?" He gently patted the cat's head. Sky rubbed against his legs and began purring and circling until he was next to Lace. The two cats touched noses through the mesh to greet one another.

"Hi Papa," purred Lace. "I'm happy. Is everyone else safe and okay?"

"Yes, and it appears you are too," Sky replied.

"I miss all of you..."

Love bent down and picked Sky up. "Hey handsome, you're lookin' good. I'm happy you came to check on Lace. Anna, your Mistress at the farm, called to tell me Lace is from your first litter. Please know we're honored to have her and you're free to visit whenever you want. She's doing fine, so no worries there."

Sky rubbed Love's chin with his head and relayed a 'thank you' to her. 'Brittany will be okay in time. She's stubborn, but I know Lace is winning her over. We wanted Lace to be with you from the beginning.' With that said, Sky jumped out of Love's arms and disappeared into the trees.

Man watched the scene between his wife and Sky. "I don't believe that just happened. Really Love, did you set this up?"

"No, but that was sweet. It's all fine. Let's get Lace inside. I'm sure it's no coincidence that Sky appeared just as we arrived. He is her dad after all."

"I agree," said Man. "It's all good." He put his arm around his wife's shoulder and they went inside with Lace.

As they entered the Vet's office, Lace couldn't help herself. She started hissing and spitting as soon as the hospital smells attacked her nose. "Get me out of here!" she screamed.

Toezer the Vet Cat expected as much from Lace. He had watched the parking lot scene with Sky and was waiting by the front door when Lace was wheeled in. He immediately moved towards the kitten to calm her down, but Love was one step ahead of him.

"It's okay Lace," the woman scooped the kitten up out of the carrier and held her firmly in her arms. "No one is going to harm you. You will leave with us, I promise."

Toezer began to meow, gaining the woman's and Lace's attention. "Well, look who else has come to greet us," laughed Man, shaking his head, quite amused.

Love smiled and placed their kitten on the floor. Lace immediately ran over to 'Toezy', as she liked to call him. "Hi Toezy, I'm alive and healthy!"

"Yes, I can see that. You gained a bit of weight too. Purrfect. I hear your name is Lace. It suits you down to the 'sss' at the end of your name. Like hissing, do ya?"

"Yesss, it's expressive." Lace said, circling Toezer.

"Good, now get back in your carrier and let's get you checked out and home quickly. I hear you and Brittany are getting along. I'm happy for you Lace." Toezer licked the top of the kitten's head a few times and swatted her into her carrier. "Stay calm, I'll be with you the entire time you're here. Good luck and regards to Britt."

"Okey Dokey, Toezy, I'm fine. Thanks. You're my hero ya know..." Love rolled Lace into an exam room. Toezer followed, keeping his word to stay with Lace.

"I don't believe this," said Man.

"I feel the same way," Love smiled. "But it's heartwarming all the same."

Lace made it through her medical exam with flying colors. The doctors and staff were impressed with how healthy she was. Best of all Lace now weighed a respectable 2.2 pounds.

As Lace left the Vets in her carrier, she spotted Sky on the edge of the lawn. She sent him pussycat kisses by opening and closing her eyes, lovingly.

Sky pranced and jumped around a few times. Love and Man spotted Sky. This time the parking lot echoed with their laughter.

Sky once again vanished into the trees. Lace was so happy to be out of the hospital. She did a flip and meowed, "Yessss!"

Later that evening, Love and Man sat out back, watching the sun set, and enjoying their ritual of 'happy hour'. They were having cocktails and nibbling on shrimp, guacamole, cheese and crackers with their two cats close by.

Both cats enjoyed the tasty morsels of shrimp their folks had given them.

Lace sat near Brittany. "Britt, my Dad and Toezer both send their greetings to you."

"It's great you got to see them again. I'm happy you got cleared by the Vet. Best of all is that you gained over a pound in a month!"

"Yesss I did, Britt the Kit, who is loved and adored by all who know her." Lace started to purr and batted a piece of her shrimp over to her best friend in the whole wide world.

"Thanks, Lace." Brittany accepted Lace's gesture and ate the pink prize. "Who told you to call me that?"

"Nathanial did. He also told me to say…"Looks like this tale has a happy ending. Oh, and he said to tell you that you're going to begin the process of becoming an Elder. Britt, what's an Elder?"

Brittany's green eyes turned gold as she watched the sun set and slip down through the distant trees, making way for the moon's light and twinkling stars to appear. She thought for a moment about the Elders she'd met over the years. For the most part they were teachers. Each one had their own special skill. They chose to unite and to use their life experience to care for all the creatures that lived in the community.

"Elders are very honest and smart, Lace. They are strong and capable, and work together to resolve situations that come up in the area. Everyone respects and listens to them, and obeys their judgments.

They solve problems, like saving your litter and getting you here, where you were destined to be. Nathanial is a 'thinker', Carlos is a 'doer', and Henry is a 'manager', so together they're a team and make life better for everyone."

"Now you're going be one, too, Britt." Lace purred. "I'm lucky, because I get to live with you."

'I wonder,' Lace mused. 'What is Brittany's special skill going to be?'

A cascade of different emotions and feelings came over Brittany all at once. She would be honored to be an Elder. Love sensed her uneasiness and picked her up, held her tight, and told her, "Life is good Brittany and your adventures with Lace have only just begun. You are a most impressive feline."

-The End Of This Sweet Tale-

SKY'S KITTENS
SAFE & SETTLED

CHAPTER ONE

"Brittany, wake up," pleaded Lace in a soft whisper. The pure white kitten was snuggled in bed with her new sister and their folks, Love and Man, in their apartment high above New York City. It was a spacious one bedroom on the upper eastside of Manhattan with lots of windows that faced north. The outside views of apartment buildings and tenements with their occasional rooftop gardens, and brownstones with enclosed backyards were in great contrast to the country's lush green trees, lawns, and fields, outside the windows of their country home.

Love and Man had brought Lace home to their country house in early summer. Brittany had welcomed and cared for Lace as well. The family divided its time between a home in the country and an apartment in New York City. Lace had quickly adapted to both places. She was quite happy and content living and traveling with her new family.

Lace didn't want to disturb the two sleeping humans who had saved her and given her a wonderful life, but she had an important question for Brittany that couldn't wait another minute. She slowly placed her paw on her sister's sleeping face, purred, and then released one claw and gently scratched the length of Brittany's long thin nose. She behaved cautiously. When she'd previously attempted this move, Britt, an orange and white ginger queen, had instinctively woken up, whopped her in the head, and sent her flying off the bed.

Lace knew they would soon be heading back to the country. A trip was planned to visit the farm where she was born and where her parents, brother, and sisters still lived. Until now, Brittany had kept Lace up-to-date on how her farm family was doing. Sky, Lace's father, had visited Lace and Brittany at their home a few times as well.

Britt felt Lace's claw, heard her purr, and knew exactly what she wanted. Lace wanted to know when they were going to the farm. What Lace didn't know, because Brittany hadn't told the kitten yet, was that one of Lace's sisters was having a hard time at the farm. Brittany was going to try to put a special plan into action to help her.

This would be Brittany's first big assignment, the first step to see if she was truly ready to become a country Elder. Although she felt skittish, she was determined to succeed. Thankfully, Britt had a great city friend in Sam, the tomcat that lived next door. She would seek him out for advice as soon as possible.

Brittany opened her eyes to see Lace's face inches away from her nose. When Lace saw Britt's eyes start to open, she gave her sister's nose a lick with her little pink tongue, then moved away quickly. Britt began to purr, letting the white kitten know she wasn't going to be smacked this time.

"Morning Lace," Brittany said, as she yawned and stretched her long thin body. "We're going to the country tomorrow and we'll definitely visit the farm this weekend."

"Yessss!" exclaimed Lace and nearly jumped out of her skin.

Love began to stir. The cats immediately jumped off the bed and ran out of the bedroom.

When Love opened her green eyes, the cats were already gone. 'I wonder what woke me,' she thought to herself. She stretched a bit and rolled over to snuggle next to her husband. As she moved toward him, she glanced over to check the time on the clock on his night table. 'Good, it's still early.' She almost started to purr herself, as she gently kissed the back of her husband's neck, and happily went back to sleep.

Brittany trotted into the kitchen, took a drink of water, and ate some cat food left over from the night before. She used the litter box and then headed to the living room where she found Lace patiently waiting for her on the couch.

Lace allowed Britt time to settle into the upholstered chair next to the couch, which happened to be one of the ginger cat's favorite places in the apartment. When Britt finished giving herself a bath, she looked up and acknowledged the adorable white kitten. Britt was amazed at how Lace had doubled in size since she'd become a part of their family.

"This is going to be a big weekend for both of us," Britt said, as she circled the chair's cushion several times before lying down and facing Lace.

"I know. We are going to Anna's farm and I am going to see my Mama and Papa, and Coco, Willa, and Scamp and Bert too!"

"Yeah, that's all true Lace, but there's more to it than that." Brittany said.

"What Britt?" The kitten inched closer to her sister, sensing something important was coming.

"It seems your sister Coco has allergies. Do you know what allergies are?"

"Yes, I do. My Mama Chayne has them, too. That's why she lives in the house with Anna. When she's outside, she sneezes a lot and gooey stuff comes out of her nose and eyes. She's not happy when that happens. Mama suffered a lot when we were born, because she had to stay in the barn with us to feed and take care of us. We couldn't all be in the house."

"Well that helps me out." Brittany was relieved. She'd had no idea how she was going to explain Coco's problem to Lace.

"Why did you ask me about allergies, Brittany?"

"Coco has developed these allergies and she's not happy on the farm. She also has a big problem with bugs, and bees, and especially hay. So, because of the way she feels, it's hard for her to be nice to anyone, including your family. She's a mess. Willa still isn't healthy, so she has to stay in the house with your Mama. Anna's also taken Bert into the house, so there's no room for Coco."

"That sounds like Coco. She's a very fussy feline and she's got some funny ways about her, but we always got along. You can't help who you are, can you Britt."

Brittany was amazed. Lace was actually turning out to be quite an asset. She closed her eyes for a moment and sent up a silent, 'Thank you, Earth Mother.'

"Okay Lace. You just made my life a lot easier. Do you want to help me find a good home for Coco and pass my first test to become an Elder? Together we can give this tale a happy ending."

"Sure Britt, I'll do anything for you. I love my life and I have it because of you."

"Great! No questions until I'm done, okay? Here's what we have to do, and please just listen for now."

"Okey Dokey, Britt."

Lace sat up and listened to Brittany's ideas of how, with the help of Sam the tomcat that lived on their floor, on the other side of the elevators, the problem could be solved.

Brittany then explained that she had briefly talked to Sam about Coco's situation and would now seek his help in identifying the 'one' Coco could have a purrfect life with. With Sam's help, Coco might be placed with one of their New York City neighbors, maybe even on the same floor.

CHAPTER TWO

Brittany and Sam were long time friends. They hung out together in the hallway and sometimes in each other's apartments. Sam's family consisted of a husband and wife and two boys. Sam's boys knew Brittany and Love, but their parents did not know Love and Man.

The two cats shared similar colors. Britt was an orange and white ginger cat, with a distinctive white blaze under her chin and a long ringtail with a white tip. Sam's markings were softer. His fur was silkier, a lighter golden brown with an orange tinge. He had pure white fur on his belly that traveled up his body, face, paws, and tail in beautiful swirling patterns. He was a handsome, formidable gent.

When Brittany first told Sam of Lace's tough beginnings, about how she and her litter had been stolen and taken to a pet store, he became quite agitated. He told her he'd spent time at a pet store in Manhattan with his brother when they were just six weeks old. He knew how lucky he was to have found a home with his loving family.

Sam was known as the 'guardian of the floor'. When he left his apartment, his routine was to check out the hallway. He'd move from one apartment to the next. He would sniff under each door until he was satisfied everything was okay. Since the hallway was quiet most of the time, his family would leave a sneaker in the doorway of their apartment, keeping the door open when they were home so he could come and go as he pleased.

After his inspection, Sam would settle across from the elevators on the soft carpet against a warm wall, behind which a large hot water pipe ran the length of the twenty-one story building. This was one of his favorite places. It was warm and cozy and he could watch everyone's comings and goings on their floor.

Sam was a few years older than Brittany. He was very fond of the young queen and enjoyed her company, most of the time. However, in the last few weeks, she'd been driving him crazy about her new sister, whom Sam hadn't yet met, and about another kitten, Coco, who needed a home.

Later that morning Brittany managed, accidentally on purpose, to get herself locked out of their apartment, in order to meet with her neighbor.

Sam heard Brittany meowing outside his apartment door. A few moments later he came out. The cats approached one another. Sam could tell by Brittany's scent that she was tense. They greeted by touching noses, then circled and rubbed against each other, as is the custom between friendly cats.

Brittany noticed that Sam was in a lousy mood, but she was determined to resolve Coco's problem. She wanted Sam to commit to helping her. "So Sam, do you remember I told you there is a situation with one of Lace's sisters?"

"Yes, I remember," he replied as his tail began to swish...

"Well, I need your help," Britt's tail was swishing now too...

"What is it you need help with, Brittany? I have no patience today."

"I need to find a home for Coco, Lace's sister and..." Britt nervously started to scratch her neck with her hind paw...

"Have you looked? What have you found?" Sam's fur began to puff and his tail swished faster.

"No, I don't know how or who, I was hoping..." Britt instinctively began to react to Sam's body language and her fur began to puff, too. The two cats were beginning to spiral out of control. Britt lowered herself to the carpet and deferred to the older cat.

Sam growled, "Why are you cowering?"

"I am not cowering Sam. You are starting to get angry and I didn't do anything."

"Really? You've been doing this for weeks now. Dancing around the issue, whatever it is, and not getting to the point," he grumbled.

"But..." Britt sat up.

"That's better. Stand up for yourself," he growled. Then he smacked Britt in the head, simultaneously hissing, 'calm down'. He too, was trying to get himself under control because he felt like he might actually attack her.

Britt got the message and sat up straighter. Sam could be ferocious if provoked too much.

"Now tell me, what is your problem? Please state it clearly and I will try to help you, or go home NOW!"

Britt sighed and settled herself. "Sorry Sam, I'm in over my head."

"Yes that's obvious. Cut to the chase. What is going on?"

"You know we live here and also in the country, right?"

"Yes, and I've traveled quite a bit myself. I've even seen an ocean."

"Really, I have not seen an ocean. But when we travel, I have seen lakes, reservoirs, and rivers. You do know Manhattan is an island so we have to go on bridges over water?"

"Yes. Stay on task. Is your kitten okay? What is her name? When will I meet her?"

"Her name is Lace and I will bring her out today." Brittany hesitated for a moment. "So Sam, Lace has a sister who can no longer live on the farm where she was born. I've been given the assignment to find her a new home soon. If I'm successful, I'll be one step closer to becoming an Elder in our country community."

"An Elder! That's very cool, Britt. There are Elders in

the city, too. Did you know that?"

"Yes, I met one when Jade and Blackie the Deli Cat took me to Central Park."

"I've been to the park with my boys. It's a beautiful place, and the creatures in the park community are, for the most part, civilized and fun."

"I agree," Brittany said. "But, as you said, let's stay on task. Please Sam, this kitten Coco needs a home. Do you have any ideas for me? Do you know anyone who wants a kitten?"

"I thought they'd all wound up in a pet store? As you know I was once in a pet store too, with my brother. Horrible places! There should be a law against them."

Brittany explained that the animals in the pet store had been rescued. Sam understood and nodded.

He seemed far away for a few moments, and then asked, "Brittany, I'm confused about one other thing. I don't get this sister thing? You say Lace has a sister Coco. You refer to Lace as your sister, so why isn't Coco your sister too?"

"Oh, I can explain. It's these human labels. Lace and Coco are real sisters, born together in the same litter, with the same parents, at the same time, along with another sister Willa and a brother Scamp. But Lace has now come to live with us, and when humans bring home more than one pet, they are considered brothers or sisters, too. So that's why Lace is called my sister."

"Okay. Got it. Now let me ponder your problem. I hear an elevator coming and I believe it will stop here. I'm expecting Carlo. He's due back from a play date with a friend. Do you want to come into our home?"

"No, I'm good, thanks. I'll bring Lace out later."

The elevator door opened. Love, and Carlo, Sam's youngest family member, exited the elevator. Carlo was a cute young boy, around nine years old, with sandy blond hair. He immediately ran to Brittany and then Sam to say hello and pet their heads. "Hi, it's really pretty outside," he told the cats.

Love said hello to Sam, gave Carlo a kiss on the head, and wished him a good afternoon. She then turned her attention to Brittany, who was sitting near Sam.

"Got locked out again, Britt? Sorry we can't install a cat door here, like the one we have in the country. Let's get you inside."

Britt ran to their apartment door and waited for Love to unlock it. Once the door opened, before Britt could run in, Lace ran out.

The little white kitten stopped short and freaked out when she saw not only Love and Britt, but Carlo and Sam. "Uh oh!" Her first instinct was to puff out, hiss, and spit at everyone.

Love immediately picked her up, and Carlo quietly moved closer. He was a sensitive boy and understood how to approach an animal. He stopped next to Love and extended his index finger so the kitten could smell it. Lace smelled something salty and gave it a lick.

Whispering, Carlo said, "You're so pretty and so white.

I'd like to be your friend." He then bent down to Britt and petted her head. "See, I'm friends with Brittany. I won't hurt you, ever. I promise."

"It's okay Lace," Love said, "you're safe. I'm going to put you down now." The woman studied the kitten. Brittany moved closer, so Lace knew she'd be protected.

Once Lace was released onto the soft carpeting she began to purr, trying to calm herself. Carlo bent down and helped her by gently moving his hand across the soft fur on her back.

Sam meowed, reminding everyone he was still there. When he started to move closer to Lace, the kitten hissed. Britt gave her a firm yet gentle pat on her tail. "Respect your elders," Brittany cautioned.

Lace got the message and proudly pranced over to Sam. She went up on her hind legs and touched Sam's face with her paw.

Although stunned, Sam remained still, since Love and Carlo were there. If they weren't, he might have reacted differently, expecting the kitten to show him more respect, since he was older and a tomcat.

"Hi, I'm Lace," she purred and sat down in front of the larger handsome cat.

"Pleased to meet you," Sam purred in spite of himself. The kitten was enchanting. "I will see you later." He then turned and padded towards his apartment with Carlo right behind him.

"Bye," Carlo yelled, as he and Sam entered their apartment.

65

Britt and Lace ran to their apartment with Love right behind them. Once inside, the cat and the kitten ran to the bedroom and jumped onto the bed.

"You were out in the hallway a long time before I came out, Brittany. Are you okay?" asked Lace.

"I'm fine. Come out later and I'll properly introduce you to Sam. He's agreed to help us with Coco."

"How can he help? And why did Love call that boy Carlo? He doesn't look like a bird?" asked Lace.

When Brittany was younger and known as 'Britt the Kit' she'd always wondered why everyone tried to duck her questions. Well, now Britt knew why. Evidently, kittens were born curious. Britt knew she must have driven everyone nuts, especially Jade. She had certainly asked a lot more questions than Lace. 'If I am going to be an Elder,' Britt thought to herself, 'I am going to have to learn to be patient and do it with an open heart.'

"Lace, listen please. The Carlos we know is a crow. He's a bird. Carlos is his name. Car-lo is a young boy, and Car-lo is his name. His Dad is from Milan in Italy. Carlo is an Italian name.

Britt held up her paw to stop Lace from asking her a question. "Wait, before you say any more. Both of us are cats. Our names are Brittany and Lace. The fact that their names are similar is just a coincidence."

"What's a coincidence, Britt?" asked Lace.

"The word 'coincidence' means by chance or happenstance. The coincidence here is just that the

66

sounds of their names are similar. It has nothing to do with who they are or what they are. Carlos is a crow and Carlo is a boy.

Lace thought for a few seconds then asked, "But it's weird, right, this 'happer stance?' Did I say it right?'

"Almost, the word is pronounced 'happen' then 'stance'... Happenstance, got it?"

Lace slowly repeated, "Happenstance."

"You did it! Well done."

Lace was pleased with herself. But then she was confused again. "Britt, how can Sam help my sister Coco? Wait, is Coco really coming here? Will she live with usss?" Lace hissed, suddenly worried that Coco might live with her family.

"No, she will not live with us, I promise. Actually, I'll guarantee it. But tell me something. Would it be okay if she lived in our building, maybe on our floor with someone else?"

"Yes, I could live with that," Lace answered as she moved closer to Brittany. "You're good to me Britt. If I asked my folks or Bert these questions they would get fidgety and annoyed, and I would feel uncomfortable. But not with you, thanks."

"It's easy with you Lace, you're smart." Britt said and sighed. "I think I need to nap now."

"I'm hungry," the kitten took off towards the kitchen.

'She's always hungry,' thought Brittany. 'I wonder why? Dinner isn't for a couple of hours.' Britt was worn out, but still determined to complete her assignment. She would do what had to be done, which was to find Coco a home. Brittany, happy to be left alone on Love and Man's bed, slipped between the soft blanket and sheets, curled up, and drifted off into a much needed catnap.

CHAPTER THREE

Later that evening, Britt, Lace, and Sam were once again together in the hallway.

Lace apologized to Sam, explaining that she meant no disrespect when they met earlier. "Sam," she asked sweetly, "Will you give me a second chance?"

Sam was quite taken with the little kitten. "Of course Lace," said Sam. "But no need for another chance, sometimes I don't react as I should either. I get bristly and I'm not as understanding as I should be. You are a delightful kitten. Let's just start fresh and leave this afternoon behind us. Does that work for you, little one?" Sam touched Lace's nose.

"Yes, it does. Thanks, Sam." Lace touched his nose in return.

"Okay you two," Brittany cut in. "This is getting mushy. We have a problem, namely Coco. Sam, have you come up with any ideas?"

"I think so. Carlo and I napped together this afternoon," Sam replied.

"The boy and I are bonded, so we communicate easily. Lace, he thought you were adorable and lovely. Britt, other than me, you are his favorite playmate. He wants to help Lace's sister and will do whatever we need him to do. He suggested Coco come live with us, but it's out of the question. Our apartment is too small for two cats."

"The truth is you don't want another cat in your home anyway." Brittany was anxious about completing her mission. "Time is running out."

"Chill out Britt. You need to be patient. Carlo let me know that our neighbor, Robin needs a pet and he prefers cats to dogs. Once he meets Lace, the boy feels things could easily work themselves out for Coco."

"How can I help, Sammy?" purred Lace. "And who is Robin? Aren't robins birds? Never mind, it must just be a coincidence."

Carlo slipped out of his apartment. "Hi, can I hang out with you?"

Lace ran over to the child and allowed him to pick her up. 'Carlo is special,' she thought, 'and I like him very much.' Lace snuggled her head into his neck and began to purr.

"There's nothing as soft as a kitten." Carlo smiled as he hugged Lace.

From around the corner of their floor's hallway, they heard an apartment door opened, closed, and locked with a key. Lace grabbed Carlo's shirt, but was careful not to scratch or dig her sharp nails into his skin.

Britt and Sam sat side by side and waited to see who would appear by the elevators.

"Well good evening," said a slim, trim, well-dressed, handsome man.

Carlo whispered to Lace, "It's okay, it's Robin. He lives here and is very, very nice. You'll like him, Lace. I promise." Lace relaxed in the boy's arms.

Brittany ran over to greet Robin. Sam stayed still. Carlo walked carefully toward Robin. "Hi Robin, we have a new addition to the floor. Meet Lace, she lives with Brittany. Please move slowly so she doesn't scratch me."

"Hi there," said Robin, bending down to take a look at Lace. "You are pretty. Brittany, your folks keep telling me I should have a kitten of my own. Carlo, do you think she'd let me hold her?"

"Lace, let him, please," purred Brittany. "He won't hurt you. Do it for Coco and me." The kitten allowed herself to be passed from the boy to the man.

Lace truly tried to control herself. She didn't like being passed around, but she'd promised to help Coco find a new home. She realized this could be an important moment. If Robin liked her, maybe he'd want Coco for himself.

When she was safely tucked in Robin's arms, she thought, 'He seems nice,' then gave his hand a sniff, 'and he really smells good, too.' When she looked up at his face, she immediately noticed his eyes. They were very kind and, 'Oh', she purred, 'they twinkle. Oh yes, I can do this.'

Carlo watched the interaction between Robin and Lace. "Hey Robin, be gentle with her, she can go from kitten to polar bear in a nanosecond," Carlo cautioned. The young boy also understood this 'meet and greet' needed to be perfect.

The man held Lace gently, lifting her so they were face to face. The white kitten was cupped in his two agile hands. Because she felt comfortable and safe, she sent him a pussycat kiss by slowly opening and closing her green eyes. Robin smiled and tucked her into his arms. He was smitten with the kitten.

"Wow she's lovely. Anymore where she came from?" Robin's smile seemed to light up the hallway. Carlo squeezed his eyes closed tightly as a 'YES' exploded inside his head.

Sam grinned from ear to ear and thought to himself, 'Yes, this will work out well.'

Brittany couldn't believe her luck! She screamed and jumped straight into the air. 'But how,' she wondered, 'was she supposed to tell him about Coco?'

As fate would have it, Love's head popped out of their apartment door. Their home happened to be near the elevators.

"Is everything okay out here? Oh, hi Robin, I see you met Lace. Quite a charmer isn't she?" The pretty lady moved toward the group. Brittany couldn't stop meowing.

Sam was amused, but didn't move a muscle.

"She certainly is," Robin replied, as the kitten snuggled closer to him.

Carlo seized the opportunity to plead for Coco, "Robin," Carlo began, "Lace has a sister that needs a home. Do you think she could live with you? It would be fun to have two kittens growing up here. Please…"

Love agreed. "Carlo is right, Robin. Lace has a couple of sisters that need homes. Are you ready for a kitten? It would be so good for you to have another heartbeat in your home."

"I know, you've been telling me that," Robin answered, "but even though my studio apartment is spacious, it's still just one room. And, I travel so much. It wouldn't be fair to the kitten."

"Don't be silly. We're all close by. Our floor is like one big happy family. Not only that, the kitten could travel with you. We do it all the time, have for decades. Cats are very self-sufficient, you know. Your pet won't mind where it is, as long as it's safe. Lace's sisters do need good homes, especially the one named Coco."

"Coco! As in Coco Chanel?" Robin laughed. He gently placed Lace on the carpet and moved closer to Love. His interest was piqued.

'Who's Coco Chanel?' wondered Carlo, 'Oh well, I'd better keep quiet and let the grownups talk…'

Love smiled warmly. "Not exactly, Coco as in the color cocoa. But, I'm sure the French fashion designer Coco Chanel would certainly have been pleased to have the kitten as her namesake. Chanel once said, 'In order to be irreplaceable one must always be different'. Coco fits that description. She is beautiful. Her fur is pure silk, white with delicate patches of cocoa and pearly grey. She's adorable and fun like you, and I think you'd be perfect for one another.

"Coco has developed allergies and cannot remain on the farm. Unfortunately, there's no room for her in the manor house, and she needs to be an indoor pet. Robin, I'm getting goose bumps."

"Yeah Robin, it's a good fit." Carlo pleaded, "Will you give her a home? She'd be near Lace, Britt, Sam, and us too. She wouldn't have to be alone in a strange place."

Love took a deep breath and contemplated the situation. She knew if she was too insistent, Robin would back off. He'd become as skittish as a cornered cat.

"Wait a minute," Love paused, "I don't want to push you. This is all part of a problem we are trying to resolve up north that involves a pet store. The owner is a very bad man."

"It's okay, you're not pushing me. I heard about how you wound up with Lace and I'd love to help. It must've been rough on the innocent animals. Let me think about it. Do you have any pictures of the kitten, 'Miss Coco Chanel'? I love the name, color or not."

Love was delighted. "No, but I'll call my friend Anna, who owns the farm where Coco is staying, and have her email some pictures right away. Thanks Robin.

"Oh, and Robin, please know that the animal hospital is not going to charge for initial medical expenses like vaccines. This will be the case for all the animals rescued from the pet store." Love went on, "And they are making sure that the animals are healthy before they are allowed to leave the farm. Anna will be pleased to give you Coco. Oh dear, I'm sorry, I guess I'm getting too excited."

"No, it's fine. You're getting me excited, too. I have to run to a dinner date. Can we talk in the morning? If I decided to give it a try, could you bring her down when you come back? And... if it doesn't work out, could she go back to the farm?"

Brittany crumbled onto the carpet. Sam growled. Carlo moaned. Lace went over to the large man and sat on one of his shoes. Love remained silent.

"Did I say something wrong?" asked Robin. He couldn't help but notice how everyone's demeanor had changed.

"No," was all Love said, and she took a moment to think this through. She really cared about Robin. They'd been neighbors for years. He was a good man who was accustomed to living alone. It was obvious he was interested and intrigued by the idea of Coco, but would he really be happier with a cat?

Carlo spoke cautiously. "Robin, it would be unfair to just try her out. She's been traumatized enough. If you want her, that's great. If not..."

Love cut Carlo off. She knew the boy was right, but wanted to keep the situation positive. "Robin, let's do this. Go on your date. I'll send Coco's pictures to you. Sleep on it, and we'll talk in the morning, okay?"

"Sure," he was confused, especially when he looked

down at the three cats staring up at him. They actually looked disappointed. "Are you sure I didn't say something wrong? These cats don't look happy with me."

Brittany meowed and rubbed against his legs, which did make him feel better, except for the fur she left on his pants.

"Okay," he sighed, "I'm sorry I have to run. I'll look at the pictures when I get home."

"Good," said Love."Let's have coffee in the morning, around nine. Does that work for you?"

"Sounds like a good plan, and Coco sounds delightful. You just may have hooked me into finally getting a cat. Thanks." Robin pushed the down button and waited for the elevator. Love kissed his cheek and waved when the elevator door closed.

Love then turned to the curious cats and Carlo. "I don't know, maybe." Love shrugged her shoulders, "Time will tell this tale."

"What happens if he decides he doesn't want her? Can Coco go back to the farm?" Carlo asked. He was visibly upset.

"Carlo, I promise, I won't let anything bad happen to Coco." Love then hugged her young neighbor. "No worries please, we'll know Robin's decision in the morning. Okay?"

"Yeah, come on Sam, I'll give you some treats. Bye, Britt and Lace, have fun at the farm." Sadly, Carlo and Sam returned home.

Love headed to their apartment with Brittany and Lace

at her heels. As soon as the door opened, her two cats ran inside.

Later that night when the elevator door opened, Robin stepped out and spotted Sam in his usual place. "Hi Sam, have you been waiting for me?"

Sam meowed and sat up. Robin moved toward the handsome tomcat and sat down on the carpet next to him. "Got something on your mind, pal?"

Sam started to purr. The two males sat together as they had done on many occasions. Together they would sort out the destiny of Coco Chanel.

At nine the next morning, Robin knocked on the door of his neighbor's apartment. Man opened it and greeted Robin, "Good Morning, you're right on time." Man had on shorts and running shoes. He was training for the New York Marathon and planned to go for a run in Central Park after their visit with Robin.

"Good morning!" Robin responded pleasantly.

"I hope you're not being pushed into giving Coco a home?"

"Not at all, I actually just got back from a pet supply place. I bought kitten food and a water fountain like yours so Coco will have cool running water. While I was there, I picked up a litter box, a bag of litter and a poop scooper. Oh, I also got a kitten brush and comb, and quite a few toys."

"Wow, sounds like you've made a decision."

"Yes I have." Robin then reached down to the floor

beside their door and picked up a soft, light grey kitten carrier, "And, with this I should have all I need to get started, right? I figure since I've taken care of your cats and Sam, I pretty much know what to do."

"Yes, you have all the right supplies, and you certainly do know what to do"

"Oh, I forgot, I also have a donation check for your animal hospital. You'll just have to tell me who to make it out to. Maybe they have a fund for helping animals that are rescued like yours, I mean ours. I'm really getting excited about all this."

Man smiled, "Yes I can see that. I think it's great for both you and Coco. I've met her. She's very pretty and likes to please."

"I can hardly wait to meet her myself. You're driving north today? When can you bring her to me?"

"Come on in! Let's have a cup of coffee and we'll figure it out."

"Great," Man stepped aside to let Robin inside.

When Love saw Robin and spotted the cat carrier in her husband's hands she smiled. "Morning, Robin, I can see by the look on your face, you're about to let a kitten share your life. I'm happy for you, neighbor."

"Thanks, I'm sorry about last night," Robin began apologetically, "the part about you taking Coco back to the farm if I changed my mind. It wouldn't be fair to do that to her. I sorted the whole thing out with a friend last night."

Handing Robin a cup of hot coffee, Love answered.

"Don't worry. We understand. It's a big decision. You'll be accepting responsibility for Coco's care for a long time. It's not just taking care of a neighbor's pet for a short period of time.

"Robin," Love continued, "the best part is you'll have each other. You'll share your home and bond with Coco, loving and caring for one another. It's going to bring you both a lot of joy and happiness."

"I know and I'm thrilled about it, if you haven't noticed."

"I'm so pleased. I heard you two talking," she gestured to Robin and her husband. "In answer to your question, we're heading north this afternoon and we'll bring Coco back with us on Monday morning. When I called Anna at the farm she was delighted. Coco has been cleared by the Vet and is quite healthy, except for her allergies. She should be fine once she's in your apartment and remains an indoor cat."

"That's good news. Thanks Love." Robin gave her a hug. He also shook hands with Man. "Wow, this is serious stuff!"

Love could have laughed or cried, but she pulled herself together. "When we get back to the city, I'll bring Coco right to your apartment so that she'll know that she's yours and your apartment is her new home."

"Coco Chanel, home! I love it!" Robin was overjoyed. "By the way, the pictures you sent of Coco last night sealed the deal. She's lovely! Her coloring is so unique, and to top it off, her mid-leg longer white fur is just like the Clydesdale horses. You were right. She's the one for me!"

Love reached for her cell phone while the two men chatted. She texted Carlo the good news. A few moments later they all heard Carlo yell "Yes!!!" through the walls from the apartment next door and they laughed.

Brittany and Lace were in the bedroom listening to the conversation. The cats began to purr and did a high five with their front paws.

"It's all good, right Britt, for everyone?" asked Lace.

"Yeah, I'd say it is." Brittany let out a big sigh of relief. "Lace, it looks like I can be a 'doer' as an Elder. This confirms it. I can 'do' what needs to get done."

CHAPTER FOUR

Love and Man's Pathfinder pulled into their half-moon driveway and came to a stop in front of their country home. Love got out of the driver's seat and opened the back door to let Brittany and Lace out. Once the two cats were released from their cat carriers they immediately jumped out and ran up the few stone steps that led to their home. Man opened the rear door and began unloading supplies for the weekend.

In the meantime, Love entered the house and turned off the alarm. The two cats curiously sniffed around the gardens closest to their home as they moved towards the back of the house. The weather was gloomy. Ominous dark clouds filled the sky. It was obvious a thunderstorm was nearby.

Lace followed Love into the house, jumped up on the kitchen window ledge, and then leaped onto the counter top. She sat right next to the plastic container that held their dry cat food.

Brittany was still outside, sitting on the patio's stone wall. She surveyed her land, seeking anyone or anything that might peak her interest. There was a sudden flash of lightning, followed by a rumble of thunder that startled Brittany. The smell of rain and electricity assaulted her nose. She quickly leaped off the wall and bolted into the house. Man was right behind her and followed her inside.

"Love," Man called, "we're in for a storm. The weather report was right."

"Okay," she called from the back of the house. "Are the cats in?"

"Yes, they're both here in the kitchen, waiting to be fed." Then he laughed.

"Lace is sitting on top of the dry food container and Britt's right next to her."

"That figures. I'll be right there."

"It's okay. I'll take care of their food and give them fresh water."

Lace touched Britt's nose with hers. "I don't like thunderstorms."

"It's okay. No worries, they don't last long. I'm just hoping it's clear on Monday morning when we go to pick up Coco and bring her to Robin."

"We won't go until then?" Lace moaned. "I thought we were going for a visit to the farm and I'd get to see my family and Bert?"

"I hope we go too, but it depends on the weather. We'll have to wait and see."

Lace circled and settled on the plastic container. The little white kitten was now sad. This was a new emotion for her, looking forward to something, then being disappointed.

Brittany was sensitive to her feelings. "Don't be sad, it doesn't mean we aren't going. I just don't know when."

Lace perked up. "I feel better now, thanks."

All night, thunderstorms roared through the area. The power went out a few times, but luckily not during dinner time. They all went to sleep early.

When the cats woke up the next morning, the storms were gone and it was a beautiful day. After having her morning coffee, Love called Anna. They arranged for an afternoon visit and an evening celebration. Anna told Love to bring Brittany and Lace.

The time had finally come for Lace to once again see her first home and family. Brittany was happy for her, and it was always fun to go to Anna's farm.

Britt the Kit was known by many at the farm, both by the humans and animals. They had seen her visiting on many occasions with Sky, or she'd sometimes turned up there when Jade or Nathanial would send her with a message for Henry.

When they arrived at the farm, Man and Brittany headed for the barn, while Love carried Lace towards Anna's home.

Anna's hilltop manor house was both inviting and well-kept. The countryside was gorgeous and best seen from the porch that wrapped around three sides of the house. From this high vantage point, the farm and neighboring area were visible. There were corrals near the horse stables. And, a lush vegetable garden, which included an asparagus patch. Nearby, a pretty English garden was planted with long-stemmed roses, an assortment of colorful cutting flowers, and an herb garden. There were beehives by the fruit trees.

A little further away were chicken coops near a quaint red barn.

Another view took in a beautiful gazebo, spacious enough for a party, with room to dance. There were two ponds. One was for swimming. The other, a short distance away, was larger and used for exercising horses. This pond was located near a big blue barn used for storage.

The surrounding farm area was part of a valley which included rolling hills of grass, fields of hay, and mountains that stood tall against the sky.

Lace squirmed and struggled to jump out of Love's arms. "Stay still little one, we'll be there soon enough," Love said, as she petted the kitten's head. But Lace was determined to make her escape. She made herself go limp and stayed very still. Her hope was that Love would relax and loosen her grip. Her ploy paid off. As soon as Love softened her hold, the kitten flew out of her arms and dropped to the ground. She scrambled up quickly and scooted away before Love could grab her.

Love smiled as her beautiful white kitten desperately made her way up Anna's front steps. She decided to let the kitten go free. As Love climbed the steps, her friend Anna opened the large wooden front door with its colorful stained glass window.

Lace scampered between the woman's legs and ran into the house. Lace knew her way around and headed down a long hallway to find the sun room. Anna laughed. From her point of view, Lace looked like a round ball of white fur rolling down the wooden floor.

In the sun room, Lace found Willa sleeping, nestled between several pillows. She noticed a long thin tube coming out of her sister's hind leg. It was connected to a plastic bag filled with a clear liquid that appeared to be dripping slowly into her leg.

Lace was shocked by her appearance. She knew Willa was sick but had no idea she was so frail. The white kitten approached the grey kitten. She gently jumped onto the couch where Willa the Grey was lying.

Lace instinctively started to purr and called softly, "Willa, it's me your big sister..."

Willa moved slowly, wincing in pain because of the intravenous needle in her leg. She opened her eyes to see Lace sitting next to her. The irises of her eyes appeared as pools of blue sadness.

"Ah Willa, I'm so sorry you're still sick. Are you getting better?"

"Hi Lace," Willa softly replied, "I love your new name. It suits you."

"Thanks Willa. How are you, really?"

"I think I'm better. I had an infection in my blood. The Vet was here yesterday and took some of my blood to be tested. We get results today and I hope the infection will be gone. Then they'll take the needle out of my leg and I'll be fine. Mama and Anna take good care of me and Bert keeps me warm every night.

"How are you doing, Lace? You look so lovely and happy."

"Yes, I am happy with my new family and homes. Even happier to be here and to know you're getting better and to see everyone. Do you by chance know where I can find Mama and Coco?"

"I don't know. I rarely see Coco. She's skittish when she's near me. I guess Coco's afraid she'll catch what I have, even though I'm not that kind of sick anymore. As for Mama, you could try upstairs. She may be napping in the cold room so her allergies don't bother her. She comes to see me a lot. Our Mama's so wonderful. She'll be happy to see you."

"I hope you get better soon. You gonna live here for good?"

"No, there is a really nice, pretty, blonde-haired lady that's going to take me in. I'll be a house cat with outside privileges, which is fine with me. It's not far away. Will you visit me?"

"Definitely, I promise. My new sister, my housemate Brittany, will bring me when I'm a little older, or I'll ask

Papa to show me where you live. Okay Willa?"

"Don't you mean Okey Dokey, Lace? I love how you say that. Say it now, please."

"Okey Dokey, Willa. I'll see you soon." Lace licked the top of the grey kitten's head. Then she gently lowered her head onto her sister's and silently said a prayer that Willa would be well and her blood healthy.

As Lace left the room, she could hear Willa begin to purr.

"Well hello my little pretty one," purred Lace's mother, Chayne, as she strolled down the hallway.

"Mama!" Lace went from sad to happy at the sight of her Mother.

"I missed you so much," the kitten ran to her Mama, rubbed up against her and purred and purred.

"Let me look at you for a moment." Chayne paused and studied her first born daughter for a moment. "My you've grown and you're very pretty! The name Lace suits you very well."

Chayne was a green-eyed calico cat. Her distinctive markings were muted shades of orange and brown. She had pure white fur on parts of her face, neck and belly, and she had four white paws. She was at once charming and elegant. Lace thought she was the prettiest cat in the world, and that her beauty was surpassed only by her sweet nature and gentle way of loving those she held dear.

When Lace thought about her Mother, she didn't yet realize she was describing her future self. Lace was a mixture of her parent's best traits. She would grow to be a formidable, caring feline, and always have Chayne and Sky's love and respect.

"Mama, Willa is so sick. Will she be well again soon?"

"I believe so, Sugar. Do you remember that was my name for you?"

"No, I remember that my name was Snow. Why do I have so many names?" Lace whined.

Chayne was sensitive to the kitten's confusion, "Most are nicknames darling, but Sugar is your special name. Only a special few will call you that. When they do, know that you can trust them with an open heart. Ok Sugar?"

"Yessss Mama, I'll remember. I'm so happy I live close by so I can visit you and Papa. I miss everyone, but I have a great new family. Come with me pleeease, I want you to meet my Mistress. She's here with Anna..."

"I know your Mistress Love, darling. As soon as I saw you, I knew you were destined to be with Love and Man. I knew Miss Jade as well. We're kindred spirits. Aspire to be like her, Lace. Carry on her legacy. Would you do that for me, little one?"

"Yes, Mama," Lace was amazed, "that would be an honor." The kitten stretched her neck and touched her mother's nose. She started to become emotional and changed the subject. "Did you hear Brittany may become an Elder?"

Chayne understood her daughter's feelings and allowed her to change her focus. "Yes I did, and part of Brittany's training is to solve a big problem. She was assigned to help your sister, Coco. Does that mean she's succeeded in finding her a good home?"

"Yes Mama, we did. Coco will live in our apartment building in New York City, on our floor, with a wonderful man named Robin. Robin's not a bird. That's just his name. It's a coincidence."

"I see. That's a big word for a little queen," Chayne purred. She was overwhelmed with love and happiness for the kitten. All was as it should be for her Sugar.

Lace interrupted Chayne's thoughts. "Brittany is very patient with me, and teaches me good words and proper ways to behave. I'm so happy I live with her. And Mama, Love and Man are very good to me, too."

"That's wonderful, Lace. Please remember to always watch out for Coco. I know she can be a bit difficult. But, you are very smart and I know you can handle her."

"I will Mama." Lace was pleased with herself. "Come with me to find Love. I ran away from her and I don't want her to worry, okay?"

"Lace, you go ahead. I need to check on Willa and I'll have to find Coco. She's hiding and has been since Papa told her there was a plan to find her a new home. And, I have to check with Sky, too, because Scamp hasn't been home for several days. You're staying through dinner so I will see you later."

"Yes Mama." Lace obeyed and ran down the hall to find Love and Anna.

Meanwhile, in the back of the red barn, Sky was scolding

his son, Scamp. The grey and white tiger was the first kitten born from the litter of four. Lace was second, followed by Coco and then Willa, the youngest.

"Where have you been? You truly are a scamp," growled Sky. "It's been days since you were home!" Sky was furious, but relieved his son was safe.

"I'm fine. I was hanging out with a nice family. I like it there. I have a few other places I go, too. One of the ladies called me a 'guest cat'. Do you know what a 'guest cat' is Pops?"

"Yes I do." Now Sky was amused. "To be honest with you, I've been one myself over the years, until I met Chayne. Once I was smitten, I had no desire to leave the farm, except to visit friends, or when the Elders have asked me to help out in the community.

"All right then, be a 'guest cat'. But I don't want your Ma to worry about you. So until you reach the age of one full year, is it too much to ask that you come by here at least once a week?"

"Okay, that's fair. I don't want to upset her either. I love her a lot. The farm is my true home and I think it always will be."

Scamp was antsy to be on his way. "So, can I go now or do you want to yell at me some more? I heard Lace was visiting and I've missed her, Pops. It's too bad we all can't stay together. Maybe I'll go be a 'guest cat' there too..."

"Forget about that, Scamp. Brittany won't have it. She's okay with visitors but very territorial with her family. We're done here, go find Lace. Tell her I will find her later. I have to meet with Henry and Brittany now about Coco."

"Did they find her a home? She's been a mess for months. I can't help but make fun of her. She literally can't stand herself."

"You're right son, and the answer to your question is one I want for myself. I'll let you know."

"Ok Pops. Thanks for understanding my need to see the world." Scamp was gone in a flash.

"Cool," Scamp said, as he ran to find Lace. "That was a lot easier than I thought it would be. So, Pops was a guest cat. I wonder what the story was with him and Ma. They're tight, those two. Maybe one day I'll find myself a queen and I'll settle down, but not too soon. I like being a scamp. It's funny how they picked the perfect name for me. Lace has a bunch of names... Yeah Lace, I want to see her now." Scamp meowed and meowed until he found his sister.

Brittany ran into Sky and filled him in on the news about Coco's new home, including the details of how she had accomplished her assignment. Then together they went to find Henry, who was also Bert's grandfather.

"Where are we supposed to meet Henry?" asked Brittany.

"We'll meet him at the edge of the wheat fields. Thanks again, for finding the perfect home for Coco. Knowing she'll be near you and Lace will be a comfort to both me and Chayne."

"Yeah, I agree. I hope she'll be satisfied. Lace says she

can be finicky. She won't be, if she's happy and content, right?"

"She'll be fine. Like her Mama, she's just not meant for outdoor living."

Brittany came to a stop and asked, "How did you wind up mating with Chayne?"

Sky sat down beside Brittany. "Anna calls it a love story like in olden days, whatever that means. She says it's like a love story between a cowboy and a city lady.

"Here's what happened. Anna took a trip down south to visit a friend on a ranch. While she and her friend were out horseback riding, Anna spotted a tiny calico kitten in the mud. Chayne was about to get stepped on by a cow."

"Really! What happened then?"

"Anna jumped off the horse and rescued Chayne. It was love at first sight, so she brought Chayne home with her on an airplane. Chayne was so little, Anna traveled with her inside her shirt. Chayne lived with Anna in the manor house.

"One day I spotted her lying on a sunny window seat. She was beautiful and I was smitten. I climbed up onto the porch and introduced myself. I asked her to come out, but she acted like she wasn't interested. Anyway, you know me, I'm persistent and I went back every day until she agreed to come outside. I knew she was really interested in me too, because she was always in the same place, waiting for me."

"That's neat. What happened next?"

"We'd go for walks together. I showed her around the farm and introduced her to everyone. She's a true queen,

Britt. She was charming, funny, and not afraid of anything. Then at night I would sneak into the house and we'd cuddle up together. I stopped roaming, Chayne is my heart's home and she adores me. We've been together for about a year now."

"I'm happy for you, Sky. I wanted kittens, but since that's not happening I feel like Lace is mine and I'm happy to raise her."

"She is yours, in all the ways that count. And, now you'll have both Lace and Coco to teach, train, and protect. How's Lace doing? I haven't seen her in a while."

"She's great. Only problem I see with Lace is she eats anything she can get her mouth on. I don't have any idea why she's always hungry. Love and Man certainly feed us enough."

"I think I know why."

"Why, Sky?"

"I've seen it before, and I've watched Scamp, Coco, and Willa. They all do the same thing. I asked Nathanial about it and he said...

'When a baby doesn't get enough food, something happens in his or her brain. Even if there is plenty of food around, in the back of the animal's mind, there's never enough. Because your litter was in that horrible pet store and not cared for properly, they will eat everything they can. Some animals overcome this problem, others don't. It's unfortunate for those that don't, because they get fat, which is very unhealthy and can shorten their lives.'"

"That's not good. Is there a way we can get them to understand that they won't ever go hungry again, now that they have good homes?"

"I'm trying, but it's not easy." Sky sighed. "Britt we better go now. Henry is waiting and I don't want to hear him growl." Both cats took off for the wheat field running and playing as they traveled to meet Henry, the black Lab.

Henry is an Elder in the community. He's always lived on Anna's farm, where he has taken on the role of manager of the animals. Bert, the yellow Lab pup is Henry's grandson.

"Finally!" Henry barked, as soon as he got a whiff of the two cats. "Get over here you two," he growled.

Brittany and Sky came to a dead stop in front of the Elder. "It's about time you both showed up. Brittany, how did you make out? Does Coco have a home? She's driving us all crazy around here. I'm about ready to put her out of her misery," grumbled Henry. Of course, he wasn't serious, just having some fun with these two cats that had found a place in his heart.

"Yes sir!" answered Brittany. "With the help of Lace, a boy named Carlo, and Sam the tomcat that lives next door to us in the big city, I can report Coco will go to her new home after the weekend and live with a man who will give her everything she needs. The home is neat and clean, just what she wants. She'll have me, Lace, and Sam to hang out with."

"Excellent Brittany! You did what you were assigned to do. And Sky, you worked hard to save your first litter. You have succeeded in keeping your word to get them safe and settled in good homes. Well done, both of you!"

Both Britt and Sky felt validated by Henry's words. Henry studied the two cats and admired the qualities they had both exhibited over the past few weeks. Brittany had come of age and was radiant. She had a strong sense of purpose and showed determination to succeed. Sky had shown that he was both loyal and trustworthy.

"Thanks Henry," both Britt and Sky meowed at the same time.

'Yes,' Henry sighed and thought to himself. 'It was a good day for the farm, and it's a good time to be together with friends and family, animals and humans alike.'

"Let's go join the others," Henry woofed. "We have a lot to celebrate, including the two of you..." The dog jumped up, scattering the cats. Britt and Sky ran after Henry as fast as they could, in the direction of the barbeque that was already under way.

CHAPTER FIVE

Later that evening, when the full moon was high in the sky, Chayne, Sky, Brittany, and Henry watched Lace and Scamp as they played together. The young cats' reunion was joyous. They were having so much fun chasing each other, purring, and sharing their stories.

A short distance away, near the gazebo, the invited guests and farm hands were visiting, talking, and enjoying their barbeque.

From Anna's porch, several loud barks sounded. Everyone stopped what they were doing and turned to look at Bert; the young, handsome, yellow Labrador pup. Coco and Willa were at his side. The people cheered and applauded. The animals responded, each in their own way.

Bert gently picked Willa up by the scruff of her neck and slowly proceeded down the stairs. Coco stayed close to Bert as they made their way down the walk. They didn't stop moving until they were in front of Chayne and Sky. Bert gently placed Willa down in front of her parents, while Coco ran to Lace and Scamp.

"Mama, Papa, I'm free of the needle and I feel fine," Willa proclaimed as she jumped around to show her parents.

Chayne sniffed and licked Willa all over her little body. She purred, "Yes, my darling, you are." Sky checked her out too, and Willa the Grey was in her glory as she snuggled with her parents.

The humans quietly watched the group of animals. They were accustomed to the way the animals communicated amongst themselves and knew this reunion was magical. They raised their glasses and toasted Chayne and Sky's first litter.

Lace, Scamp, and Coco watched the scene unfold with their baby sister Willa.

Coco asked Lace, "So you found me a good home and you'll be my neighbor in the city?"

"Yes," replied Lace. "We will pick you up after the weekend. I believe you will be very happy there. I will always be close by and Brittany will guide you as you grow up."

Scamp rubbed against both his sisters, "You two are beautiful. I'm so happy you'll live near each other. Coco, I know you'll be fine living in the city. Your allergies will be history!"

"Wouldn't that be nice?" mused Coco.

97

"Let's go and greet Willa," Lace said "and we'll all be together again!" The three kittens ran to their sister for a heartwarming gathering.

Bert stood near Henry as they watched the four kittens reunite. No longer were they afraid or sick, abandoned or frightened.

"Bert you did a fine job protecting and caring for those kittens. You should be very pleased with yourself." stated Henry.

"Thanks Gramps. I'm sure gonna miss them." Bert shook his head and settled in the soft grass.

"Bert, our Earth Mother has given you a gift. Now that the kittens are safe, it's time for you to move on. There's work to be done."

"There is?" Bert sat up attentively.

"Yes, you have turned out to be an 'Alpha Dog', the name for dogs that are born leaders. I have decided to prepare you to take over my job. Not any time soon, but someday you'll be the manager on this farm.

"I want you to always stay by Anna, and be by her side in the house and out. I will coach and train you, so when the time comes, you'll be ready. You'll also have additional responsibilities serving the community, as I do. My hope is that Brittany will teach, protect, and guide you when you're off the farm."

Bert felt chills run though his strong young body. He shivered and took a deep breath. Then from his floppy ears to his long tail, he shook, sending shock waves rippling through his body, and sending his fur flying in all directions. "That's a big job Gramps. I kinda like taking care of the little ones, and I have no real desire to leave the farm. Do I have to?"

Henry sniffed the air and realized it was getting late. "Bert, as you get older you'll get to the point where you'll naturally want to lead. And then there will be times when you'll know you just have to take charge. But now, let's join the litter you protected and cared for so very well."

As Bert and Henry joined the party, Bert's heart filled with satisfaction at the sight of Scamp, Lace, Coco and Willa, together again with their family and friends.

At the edge of the woods, looking on, were Nathanial the Woodchuck and Toezer the Vet Cat.

"My my, this is a heartwarming sight," said the woodchuck to the cat.

"Yes, it is dear friend. That's why I invited you to come with me tonight. After all, none of this would have happened without you."

A quiet 'caw' came from a tree branch above the two animals. "What about me? Am I chicken soup or something?"

Nathanial chuckled, "No Carlos, you're not soup. You're smart, brave, and absolutely wonderful."

Carlos the Crow flew down and joined his friends, "Thank you, Nathanial. Now I feel better."

"Thanks to you, too, Toez," cawed the crow. "You did good by those kittens. Remember, you're the one that alerted Nat, in the first place, and blew the whistle on that bad 'pet store guy'."

Carlos eyed his two companions. "Let's not forget Britt the Kit. She did good, too. She graciously accepted Lace and found Coco a home."

"Okay," said Nathanial, "we've all patted ourselves on our backs enough. It's time to go home. This matter has been successfully settled." The woodchuck, the cat, and the crow disappeared into the woods.

As Lace looked around, she realized someone was missing from her family's reunion. It was Brittany. The little white queen slipped away and ran to a large rock near the barbeque pit. Once she'd jumped to the top of the rock, she willed her body and green eyes to scan the area until she found the ginger cat sitting alone near the edge of the woods.

Brittany was sitting by herself after Nathanial, Toezer, and Carlos left. She'd silently moved close to them, to listen in on their conversation, but chose to remain hidden.

The little white kitten jumped off the rock and ran towards her sister. Brittany purred when she spotted Lace bouncing up and down as she ran across the lawn.

"Brittany, what are you doing here alone? Please come and be with me Coco, Willa, and Scamp and Bert."

"That would be my pleasure, Lace. I'm happy for all of you. And most of all, I'm happy you're coming home with me."

Lace and Britt ran to the group of kittens. They welcomed Brittany with meows and pussycat kisses, rubbed against her, and filled her with joy. She was overwhelmed by the love and attention the kittens showered on her.

"Bert," whispered Lace. "Please come, and let me be with you before I have to leave." The young pup moved closer to the white kitten. "I miss you so very much. How are you?"

"I'm good Lace. I have missed you, too. But I think we will be spending more time together. My Grandfather wants Brittany to be my guide when I have assignments away from the farm."

"That sounds important." Lace snuggled under Bert's chin. Does Brittany know?"

"I don't know. Bert paused, thinking. "Maybe I wasn't supposed to tell anyone yet, and my Grandfather will have my head if he finds out. Lace, can you keep my secret for now, please?"

"Okey Dokey, Bert. You have my word."

"Thanks Lace. I can't tell you how happy I am to see the four of you together."

"We were lucky we had you Bert. With you there the whole thing wasn't as scary, so thanks big guy, I love ya!"

As Lace was licking Bert's snout, she felt soft hands reach around her belly. "Sorry little one, it's time to get you home," Love said as she placed a kiss first on her kitten's head then on the pup's head. Holding the cat, she bent down and nuzzled Bert's head between his ears. "Mmmmm, there's nothing like smooching the top of a Lab's head. Bert thanks for all your help. You're welcome at our house any time."

Lace and Bert exchanged a knowing look. Love then walked away with Lace in her arms.

Bert headed over to say goodbye to the calico cat. "Hey Coco, come here."

"Hi Bert. This was such a wonderful party. Guess you'll be happy when I move to my new home."

"Don't be like that Coco," woofed Bert. "There's no need to be smug anymore. You know I'm fond of you and I understand this whole situation has been difficult. But, now you can calm down and be grateful, darn it!"

"You are absolutely right, Bert. I'm blessed, and I thank you for everything you did for us. Please take care of Willa and Scamp. She's so delicate and he's so daring. I will worry about them."

"I will Coco. Just, please, be nice and play fair in your new home."

"I'll try Bert, really I will," Coco purred.

Chayne, Sky, and Britt were laying nose to nose, content with their success. They heard Love's voice calling repeatedly, "Brittany, Brittany. It's time to go home. Where are you? Come to me, please."

"I gotta go now." Brittany stood up and stretched from head to tail. "I'll keep an eye on Coco, don't worry. And, I'll come by next weekend to let you both know how her homecoming went." There was a flash of orange as Britt ran off to her Mistress.

"She's such a gem, Sky," purred Chayne.

"Yeah, Britt's cool. I think she deserves to be an Elder. She's been wonderful helping us get our first litter safe and settled."

"I agree and her timing's purrfect. Since, my love, our second litter is on its way."

CHAPTER SIX

Early Monday morning Love and Man's blue Pathfinder slowly pulled out of their driveway as they started out for Anna's farm. Brittany and Lace were zipped in their carriers in the back seat. Man was driving, and Love was in the front passenger seat with Coco's new carry case on her lap.

"Well," said Love, "we're on our way. I do hope this all works out for the best."

"Of course it will. "Why wouldn't it? Everything will be fine. Don't worry, be happy," Man smiled at his wife, "just like the song, Love."

"You're right." Love took a deep breath and slowly exhaled to calm herself.

As they pulled into the farm's driveway, Anna was waiting, holding Coco in her arms. Love opened the car window as her friend approached. "Morning, Anna."

Anna moved to the open window and handed Coco to Love. "Good morning to all. Here ya go, Coco Chanel on her way to the Big Apple." The kitten meowed in protest. She did not enjoy moving vehicles.

Love didn't fuss with Coco. She just put the pretty kitten in her new carrier. Robin had placed a soft, lavender scented, satin pillow in the bottom of the case. Once Coco sniffed around and felt its smooth softness, she settled down quickly, feeling content.

Love, Anna, and Man shared a laugh and shook their heads. "She's something else," commented Man.

"Looks like your Robin already knows what this one likes. Good luck to all," Anna called. She waved as they pulled out of the driveway.

The ride to the city was uneventful. Everyone was on their best behavior. Coco was comforted by Brittany and Lace's presence in the back seat. Love kept her hands gently but firmly around the carrier and the extremely quiet kitten.

When they reached their Manhattan apartment building, Love got out with Coco and headed to the front entrance. Man drove down into the parking garage in their building.

When the woman and cat reached the building, the doorman opened the large glass door and they slipped inside. Once inside, Love motioned with a finger to her lips, alerting the doorman and the building's superintendent standing by his desk, to stay still and be quiet. Both men peered in at the kitten in her carrier and admired her beauty.

Mike the Super told Love that Robin had called down, asking to be buzzed on the intercom as soon as she arrived with his new kitten. He would be waiting for them when the elevator door opened on their floor. Luckily no one else was in the elevator and they rose quickly to their destination. Coco neither moved nor made a sound. As the doors opened, there was Robin, smiling, waiting to meet his Coco Chanel!"

"Hi Robin. Look who's here!" Love showed him the kitten in the carrier.

"Hi there," he said to Coco and extended his index finger for her to sniff. He also gave Love a kiss on the cheek and asked. "How was the ride down?"

"It was uneventful and quiet, thank goodness," Love sighed. "Let's get her into your apartment before Man and the cats come up from the garage."

"Sure, follow me." Robin led the way. He held the door open to his studio apartment so Love could enter first. Love placed Coco on his couch and unzipped the top of the carrier.

"Okay Robin, turn on your charm. Coco's all yours. I suggest you sit with her and talk softly to help her get comfortable. Let her make the first move. When you see her sit up, keep talking and pet her head. Then slowly take her out of the case and place her on your lap. Coco knows her name and should respond positively when you say it."

"Right, you told me that. How does she know her name?" Robin was curious.

"It's what they called her on the farm. I assumed it's from her coloring. But now we know better, her name is Coco Chanel, and she's yours!"

Robin and Love shared a laugh.

"So," Love continued, "if Ms. Chanel gives you any

trouble, come get me. If she's okay, let her look around. Show her where her food, water, and litter box are and keep an eye on her. If you stay calm and positive, my feeling is, she'll be fine. I'll come by later. Enjoy!" Love gave him a big hug and slipped out the door."

Robin followed Love's advice. The beautiful, elegant kitten complied in every way. Within minutes, she had used the litter box, lapped up some water, and sniffed around the apartment. Satisfied, she jumped back onto Robin's lap, content with her new home.

She settled herself and then meowed softly a few times and nudged his hand with her head, asking to be touched. Robin responded by stroking her back and rubbing behind her ears and under her chin. Coco started purring softly and sweetly. Robin sighed, knowing he'd made the right decision.

When Carlo came home from school later that afternoon he ran to Robin's apartment right away, accompanied by Sam. Carlo was tickled by Coco's attention. Sam thought she was pretty, but a bit presumptuous.

After they left, Love let Lace and Brittany go for a visit. Lace approached her sister, "So Coco, how are you doing?" The white kitten sniffed her sister for clues.

"Fabulous Lace, he's perfect! I love my new home! Thanks, to you and Brittany."

Coco went over to Britt and touched her nose with sincere kindness. Brittany was shocked, but gracious.

"It's like she's a different kitten, isn't she, Lace?" Britt stated questioningly.

"Yes, that's Coco. She's a cool one."

"Lace," Coco said, "you didn't tell me about the handsome tomcat down the hall."

"You mean Sam?" Lace responded.

"Yes, Sam the man... I like him," purred Coco.

"He's too old for you, Coco." Brittany felt a blush of green jealousy. She hadn't thought about sharing Sam, not only with Lace, but Coco too. But her jealously and selfishness quickly faded. She knew that neither Lace nor Coco were a threat to her relationship with Sam.

Lace picked up on Brittany's feelings. "Coco, Brittany is right. As she's taught me, 'respect your elders', unless of course you want to go back to the farm."

"Back to the farm, never!"

As the two kittens went through their little spat, Brittany took a moment to check on her own feelings. Lace and Coco were hers to raise, protect, and care for throughout their kittenhood. Their parents Chayne and Sky had given her that responsibility and she had accepted with an open heart.

"Lace, take it easy. Coco is not going back to the farm. This is her home now. Coco, your folks asked me to watch over you, and I will. Sam is a good friend of mine and we peacefully and respectfully share our space on this floor. If you want to flirt with Sam, be my guest, but know he has a short temper and doesn't put up with nonsense. So tread lightly. Okay?"

"Yes, thank you, Brittany. I know I have some adjusting to do here. I will be respectful. Lace, you can calm down now."

"Coco, I'm happy you understand," Lace said, as she moved closer to Brittany and rubbed against her. "Let's go home now, Britt. We'll see you tomorrow Coco. I am happy you are here with us."

"Thanks Lace." Coco's last two guests of the day departed.

Still feeling a bit unsettled, Coco ran to 'her' Robin. She jumped into his lap and snuggled into his arms. Robin gently kissed her head and softly whispered, "Coco Chanel, neither one of us is alone anymore." Coco sighed, "Ah yes, finally I have a home of my own. There were times I thought I'd never belong anywhere. But here I am. I'm safe and feel content." Softly, she began to purr.

Britt and Lace trotted to their own apartment. Love had placed the usual heavy, bronze doorstop in their doorway to keep the door open, so the cats could run back inside when they finished visiting with Coco.

When Love heard the cats come home she closed and locked the front door. A few minutes later she found Brittany and Lace curled up on the oversized couch in the living room.

"Is everything okay, girls?" Love asked, as she placed herself between the cats. The cats purred and enjoyed Love's warmth. "I'd say that worked out splendidly.

Robin and Coco are smitten. I believe this tale has a happy ending."

Brittany and Lace looked at each other in disbelief. Their Mistress had just said Jade's favorite expression at the end of an adventure...

Love noticed their reaction and smiled, "Where do you think my Pussywillow learned that phrase in the first place? Jade loved a happy ending and so do I!" Love hugged her cat and her kitten. Their ears perked up when they heard the snap of the front door lock being opened with a key.

A moment later Man appeared in the living room. His heart warmed at the sight of his wife and cats. "Well, isn't this a pretty picture."

"Come join us," Love whispered.

"That would be my pleasure." As soon as Man was settled next to Love, Brittany moved onto his lap. Lace imitated her sister and moved onto Love's lap.

Just down the hall, Coco Chanel was snuggled in Robin's lap. Next door Sam was asleep beside his Mistress. In the country, Willa was settled in her new home, and Scamp was being fed his third dinner of the day. Bert and Henry were having dinner at the manor house with Chayne, Sky, and Anna. It was indeed a happy ending for all.

-The End Of This Sweet Tale-

WINTER SNOW & JUSTICE

CHAPTER ONE

It was winter, and Brittany and Lace's country home was covered in a soft powdery white blanket. Lace, a pure white kitten, was in awe of the magical flakes that fell softly onto their land.

Lace's humans, Love and Man, were sleeping peacefully in their big bed. Her sister, Brittany, a long and lanky, orange and white, ginger queen was cuddled in Love's arms.

Lace padded into the kitchen, looking for something to eat. Her cat food bowl was empty and she was struggling not to touch Brittany's food. She knew Britt would be angry with her if she ate the last few pieces of kibble left in her sister's bowl.

"I have to be strong and leave Britt's food alone," Lace declared. She knew she wasn't really hungry. Brittany had explained to her that it was just her brain playing tricks on her. "But, why do I feel so hungry and want to eat all the time?" she wondered.

"This happens to youngsters like you," Britt had patiently explained, "You were starved as a young kitten, and so you often feel hungry, even though now you have plenty to eat."

Lace remembered that empty, weak feeling she'd had at the pet store, that horrible place she'd ended up when her litter was kidnapped on their way to the animal hospital for checkups. Luckily Bert, a male yellow Lab pup, had protected the litter of four kittens when Love and Man rescued them, along with the other stolen animals. Since that time, Lace and Bert had remained best friends.

In fact, it wasn't just the humans that had saved the kidnapped animals. It was Nathanial the Woodchuck, Toezer the Vet Cat, and of course Carlos the Crow.

Brittany was very special to Lace. She had graciously accepted Lace into her home with Love and Man. Lace had since learned that Britt the Kit had also saved her father Sky when he was just a kitten.

As Lace pondered her eating problem, an evergreen tree branch hit the kitchen bay window. She jumped on to the ledge and looked outside.

"Wow, everything is so white! Just like me! It must be? Yesss! It's SNOW. Now I understand why Papa called me Snow." The white kitten got chills all over her body. "Snow is all white and pretty like me! I want to touch and feel it," Lace whispered.

The kitten ran over to the cat door which was part of the kitchen door of their house. She placed her paw on the clear plastic door and pushed. "Ah, it's open." Her folks had forgotten to lock it before they went to sleep. "Should I?" Lace knew it was the wrong thing to do, but she was so curious about the snow falling just a short distance away in their backyard. "Yes, I'll chance it. Just, for a few minutes." She took a deep breath and slipped through the flapping door.

Once outside, Lace ran to the snow and placed her paw on the sparkling white powder. "Oooo, it's cold, like Mama said. Ah, it melts too." Cautiously she moved out from under the covered porch and jumped up onto the stone wall that ran the length of their home.

As the snow gently fell on the kitten, she began to purr. It was cold, but pleasant. It landed on the top of her head and body. "So this is snow. I like it. But I like the name Lace better because of the 'ssss' sound at the end. I also like the meaning of the word 'lace'. Love showed me a white lace handkerchief," the kitten remembered, "and explained that it was delicate, but also very strong. She said it was threads sewn together into beautiful patterns."

Lace looked around at the transformation of her land into a winter wonderland. The lawn sparkled, covered with a soft white blanket of snow. The branches of the trees and bushes were trimmed in white and shimmered in the gentle wind. It was clean, beautiful, and quiet.

The white kitten took a deep breath, and when she let it out she noticed she could see her breath. It looked like clouds of smoke coming from her mouth. She blew out again and giggled, "That's fun."

"Look at you, sitting there all by yourself, just like a sugar cube. Perhaps I'll lick you and then swallow you up. Didn't anyone tell you it's dangerous to be out in winter in the middle of the night?"

Lace froze. She didn't even breathe. She was face to face with what looked like a furry grey monster with smoke fuming around its head.

Suddenly, the sound of the cat door flapping open and shut filled the air. There was a flash of orange as Brittany leapt onto the wall and landed between the two animals, prepared to protect her sister. "Don't scare her like that, she's not even a year old," protested the ginger feline.

"Relax Britt. I was just having some fun. But your kitten shouldn't be out here by herself. You're lucky it was just me passing by. She looks like she'd make a delicious plump snack," said the scrawny grey animal, showing a flash of sharp white teeth.

"Brittany, make it go away pleeease," pleaded Lace in a low hiss. "And what is it, anyway?"

"Take it easy kit. I'm not going to harm you. Everyone knows your land is off limits to hurting or harming anyone or anything. Your land is called a 'sanctuary' so you're safe, at least from me. I'm Grey-Grey and I'm a fox."

"Foxes are red and pretty. You're grey and scary! You kinda look like a dog. My name is Lace. I used to be called Snow, so since this is the first time I've ever actually seen snow, I snuck out here." The kitten then turned to Brittany.

"Sorry I woke you, but I'm very grateful you came to my rescue."

"Get inside Lace, NOW," Brittany hissed. The kitten quickly jumped off the wall and scampered into the house. "Thanks Grey for not hurting her. Looks like Earth Mother's beginning winter. You need something to eat?"

"Nah, I'm good, thanks for asking. You better go have a talk with the little one. She definitely should not be out here, especially right now. The woods are not as peaceful or pretty as they look. I think trouble's coming. Take care, Britt the Kit." The fox was gone in a flash.

Brittany sniffed the air. Her nose picked up the scent of smoke from the fireplaces in neighboring homes. It was damp, so she knew the snow wouldn't last long, and yes, she smelled it too. There was danger in the air.

Lace was waiting for Brittany when she came back into the kitchen. The kitten watched as Britt used one of her claws to move their cat door into its locked position. "Don't let on to anyone that I know how to open and close our door. Understand?"

"Yes Brittany. Are you mad at me? Are you going to hurt me? I didn't eat your food, but I couldn't resist going out to experience snow for the first time in my life." Lace meekly circled the older cat.

Britt hesitated, then jumped on the kitten and they playfully tumbled around on the floor. "Lace you need to think. Grey-Grey is a fox, which means he's a much wilder animal than a dog like Bert. He's feral and lives by his guts and instinct. If he was really hungry or angry he could rip you into pieces. Heed my warning. Know that this time next year you could get away from him, but not this winter. Got it?"

"Yes, I'm working on controlling myself, and I'm doing my best."

"I know that. In a few months you'll be bigger and stronger. You'll be safer too, especially in the snow, since it's white and you'll be invisible. How does that sound?" Britt tilted her head.

"That's cool, but the snow is cold." Do you like being out in it?" Lace nuzzled her sister's neck.

"Yeah, I do. I don't weigh a lot so usually I can make my way on top of it without falling into it and getting stuck."

"Uh, oh! What about me?" Lace's green eyes opened wide. She knew she was gaining weight every month.

"I don't know. That's up to you kiddo."

"It's that 'pet store guy's' fault that I'm always hungry! Darn, I wish I could get my claws into him someday soon!"

"Be careful what you wish for Lace. Jade tried to teach me that lesson, and I didn't listen. I learned it the hard way. Anyway, you can have the rest of my food. I'm going back to sleep." Brittany left the kitten alone in the kitchen.

"What does that mean? Now what am I supposed to do?" Lace whined. But it only took a minute for her to eat every bit of kibble left in the bowl. Then she followed Britt to bed.

The next morning, Lace couldn't believe her eyes.

The snow had vanished, the sun was out, and the sky was blue. "Britt, where did the snow go?"

"It melted. That happens sometimes," answered Brittany. "I'm glad about that because I have to go meet Bert. You stay close to the house today."

"Can't I go with you? I want to see Bert too."

"No, if we have time I will bring him by before he goes back to Anna's farm. But you stay out of the woods. Something is not right, and until I know what it is, you won't be safe."

"Okey Dokey, I don't mind, I don't want to see that Grey-Grey guy again."

Britt slipped out through the cat door and headed towards the farm. Once she entered the woods she heard movement under a pile of colorful leaves. "Who's there?"

"Hey you, how's it going," said a squirrel, as he popped up and shook off some leaves. He was cute and skinny. His fur was grey and he had a white belly. He was a youngster, born in early spring just like Lace.

"Hi One, how's it going," the cat replied.

"Don't call me that! It's not my name. It's what Love used to call me because she couldn't tell the difference between me and my brothers and sister."

"I know, she used to call your brother Two because his fur is grey and he has a white and grey ringed tail, and you don't. What happened to the other two?"

"They moved over a few houses. Will you call me Rikki from now on?"

"Yes Rikki, and I will call Two, Benny, because I know that's his name. But, can we use One and Two as code names, just in case of an emergency? We'll keep it a secret."

"Yeah, I guess I gotta listen to you since you're going to be an Elder, right?"

"Yeah, that's what they tell me, but I don't know when. Listen Rikki, I'm going to tell Lace about your code names in case she's in trouble. Tell Benny too, okay?"

"Okay Brittany. Do you think there's going to be trouble?"

"Maybe, I gotta go now." Brittany headed off through the woods to meet Bert.

CHAPTER TWO

Britt found Bert on the farm near a large pond. The yellow Labrador Retriever pup had doubled in size since she'd last seen him. Brittany watched as he was put through his paces by Henry, his grandfather, who was also an Elder.

Bert's sleek, young body was moving quickly. He was jumping and climbing on and off bales of hay, some piled as high as fifteen feet. He then circled the huge stacks a couple of times.

After that Bert dove into the exercising pond that was used mainly for horses. He swam the length of the pond, turned around, swam back, climbed out and repeated the same exercises over again. All the while Henry was critiquing his movements and speed.

'Wow,' thought Britt. 'Bert's gotten so strong and fast. Henry is a good trainer. Maybe I can get him to work out with me. Nope, that's a bad idea. He'd make me swim in the water. I'm not doing that!'

The cat sat and watched, not showing herself, until the

stately black Lab called to his grandson, "We're done here for today, Bert. We're being watched and I suspect it's Brittany, who's been waiting for you. Good workout."

When Britt heard Henry, she showed herself and moved down to the bales of hay and the pond. "Hi Henry, you sure do give a good workout session."

Bert barked in agreement.

"Good day, Britt. I'd be happy to give you one." Henry said as he pranced over to the cat. Henry was a dignified black Labrador Retriever, in good physical shape.

"No thanks, I'm good. Hi Bert, are you ready for your next round of training with me?"

"Woof woof," barked the young handsome Lab, who was dripping wet. He proceeded to shake himself from head to tail, sending a spray of water over Henry and Brittany. "Yes, just give me a minute to grab some food and drink some cleaner water."

"Okay, replied the ginger cat. "Henry, I think something is going on around here. Have you heard about anything strange?"

After Bert trotted off to the barn, Henry sat down next to Brittany.

"Yes, I'm afraid so. Today when you're out with Bert, please go to the north end of town on the lake. There is an abandoned, bright blue house where strange noises have been heard in the middle of the night. Investigate please."

"What's up," Bert said when he returned from the barn. He was dry and full of energy.

"Brittany will explain. You two have a good day, and be careful. Be very careful," barked Henry.

"Yes, Grandfather." The cat and the dog ran off in the direction of town and the far end of the big lake community.

"Lace sends her love, Bert. She saw snow for the first time last night, snuck out of the house in the middle of the night, and met a grey fox."

"Lace, really, that's pretty daring for her, isn't it?" Bert was concerned for his younger friend.

"Yeah, I was surprised, but then she's surprising," noted Brittany.

"Did the fox try to harm her?"

"No, he's a neighbor."

Britt and Bert set off for their destination. Brittany showed Bert how to go 'as the crow flies'. Carlos the Crow had explained that means to travel as crows do, moving from point A to point B in a direct line without any detours. The cat and dog took shortcuts, cutting through wooded areas and backyards, staying off the roads, and away from people. They were moving very quickly, so there was no longer time for chit chat.

When they reached the run-down community at the end of the lake, Britt looked around for the house Henry was concerned about.

"What are you looking for?" asked Bert.

"A house that Henry said is bright blue and that's been abandoned."

"What's an abandoned house?"

"It's one that's empty. No one is supposed to be living there, but your Grandfather said people have been spotted inside and animals were heard crying."

"I see," said Bert. The dog began to look around at the rundown buildings, homes, and stores. He noticed the area was littered with garbage and the yards were unkempt. The area seemed deserted and it felt a little creepy. "I've never been to a place like this. Wait, could it be that blue house down the road, on the water?"

"Good eyes, Bert. Let's go check it out. We'll make our way by the edge of the lake, okay?" Britt could tell Bert was a bit uncomfortable. "Relax big guy, this is the fun part. Not getting caught is when it gets hairy."

Brittany took off for the house in question with Bert following the white tip of her long ringtail. They were used to traveling together and easily kept in sync with one another. When Britt almost fell into the lake, the strong young pup easily saved her by putting his front paw out and batting her back to the safety of the land.

The cat meowed, 'thanks' when they reached the back of the blue house. They both just sat there staring at the house.

"What do we do now, Brittany?" asked Bert.

"We watch and wait," said the cat, and so they did. After awhile, Bert became a bit fidgety and started to scratch his neck, ears, and nose. Britt stayed alert and focused on different floors of the three story house. Most of the windows were boarded up and the blue paint was chipped and faded.

"Bert," Britt whispered, "I hear something. Be quiet and still." The ginger cat listened carefully. "There's crying coming from the second floor. Look at the broken window, the one near that big tree. It's the window with the long branch next to it."

"Yeah, it looks like there's a cat in the window. It's Scamp! What's he doing all the way over here?" Bert growled.

"Let's go see if he's okay." Britt moved quickly towards the house and the tree. Bert was still on her tail.

"This is what's going to happen now," Britt explained. "I'm going up the tree to see what's going on and you are going to stay here. If you see any people, start barking your head off. If they come after you or seem unfriendly, take off. Don't worry about me. Got it? No time for questions, pal." Brittany started up the tree. Bert did as he was told.

When Brittany got to the tree branch closest to the window, the grey and white tiger tom kitten screamed at her as loud as he could.

"Brittany, get out of here. It's the 'pet store guy'. There are a bunch of us cats, dogs, and rabbits locked up in here, in the same room, and some men just let loose a pack of wild dogs. It's crazy, but I'm okay. I'm on a window ledge next to a rafter." Britt could now hear all the animals and it sounded very scary inside.

Down below Bert started to bark and growl. Hackles of

fur rose along the dog's spine and neck. The Lab looked up at the cats. He was panicked and very angry. "It's the 'pet store guy', Britt! The last time I saw him, I lifted my leg and peed on him, just as the police officers came into the store. He's gonna kill me. What should I do?"

Before Britt could respond she saw the man coming at Bert with a baseball bat, ready to hit the pup. "Run Bert! Now!"

Bert was torn. He didn't want to leave Brittany and Scamp, but his instincts told him to run. In an instant the man was on him and slammed him with the bat.

Shocked, Brittany instinctively jumped from the tree onto the man's back and began to scream and claw him with her sharp nails. The man dropped the bat and tried to pull the cat off his back. Bert growled, bit the man's leg, then quickly jumped up, and knocked him over. Scamp watched silently from above.

"Uh, oh!" Scamp cringed, afraid to his core for the cat and the dog. "I guess I'm up." He quickly managed to climb out of the broken window and proceeded to do a free fall onto the 'pet store guy'.

The man spotted Scamp falling and saw the look in the cat's piercing blue eyes. He covered his face with his hands to protect his eyes, since Scamp was aiming right for them. The tiger kitten did a belly flop directly on target and landed on the man's face.

In an instant the two cats and the dog made their getaway. As they parted, they decided to regroup and meet at Henry's barn. The cats went by land and the dog jumped into the lake and swam away.

Once the cats were far enough away from the abandoned house, they stopped to rest. "What the heck, Scamp! How did you wind up in there?" Britt was exhausted and upset.

"My friends disappeared from one of my hang-outs and I tracked them to that house. They didn't warn me fast enough so I got locked in. I was safe enough. But I freaked when I saw the 'pet store guy'. I swear he recognized me. He picked me up, took one good look at me, and threw me against a wall. After that I just stayed out of his way and I was fine. Things are bad in that house. I won't go back there," said Scamp.

"You're nuts, you know that! Have you no sense? Where is your self-respect? You don't ever have to be in a place like that," Brittany screamed. "You have a home and a family and friends. Think about what it would do to them if something happened to you." Instinctively, Britt smacked the young tom in the head. "Come on, let's find Bert, he took a few nasty blows to his head and back from that baseball bat."

"Sure, Britt. Thanks for the advice and the right hook to my head."

Brittany noticed the tender skin between one of Scamp's eyes and ear was bleeding. "Sorry Scamp," Britt touched where she scratched him. "I didn't mean to break your skin. Let's go."

"It's nothing, I deserved it. I wonder what my Pops

will do to me when he hears about this. But this isn't about me anymore. Let's find Bert first. Then I'd like to help free my pals and all the other animals from that house, except for that pack of dogs. They're bad news. Yeah, and can we get that 'pet store guy', too?"

"Scamp, get a hold of yourself. I will tell Sky that you were very brave. We'll talk to Henry about getting everyone out of the abandoned house."

Britt was now amused with Scamp. "It's funny you said that about the 'pet store guy'. Lace mentioned getting even with him last night, too. I agree with both of you. It's time we get that guy out of here, once and for all."

The cats met up with Bert and together they went to see Henry. Bert's injuries were not serious and wouldn't require a visit to the Vet. Henry patiently listened to the three animals yapping all at once telling their tale. He was amazed by their courage, bravery, and also at the stupidity that had gotten them into trouble in the first place. But, he also realized Brittany did what she was supposed to do, Bert led with strength, and Scamp would always land on his feet.

Henry decided to seek out Nathanial and discuss the situation. They would need to come up with the best way to deal with the 'pet store guy' and put a plan into motion quickly. What the Elder black Lab didn't know, as of yet, was that the feral dogs in the blue house were working for the 'pet store guy'.

Later that same night, Henry left his barn and made his

way through the farm and up into the ring of mountains that bordered the valley where he'd lived his whole life. He didn't usually travel far from home these days, but he'd come up with a shrewd solution to quickly free the animals at the abandoned house.

Being off the farm, Henry felt liberated. He enjoyed his journey across fields, through the woods, and up the mountain. It was quiet and peaceful. The moon and stars were out and the air was cool and sweet.

Henry's body was strong, lean, and powerful. His shiny black fur glistened in the moonlight, thick and sleek as a shield or coat of armor. He had been an Elder for many years and was respected by both domesticated and wild animals in the area.

Where he was headed was not safe, but it was necessary for him to go there. If the animals in the abandoned house were to be freed quickly, he felt this was their best option. He'd made this decision on his own and would be held responsible for the outcome. Good or bad it would be on him alone.

When Henry reached the highest mountain plateau above the tree line, he howled a call to the coyotes that lived in the area and waited for a reply. A few moments later a creamy white and beige, fully furred, breathtaking coyote, stepped out from the long shadows of the surrounding trees.

"Henry! How handsome and healthy you are. It's been many moons since you graced us with your honorable presence." The coyote's fiery amber eyes scanned the black dog.

"And you're looking majestic and beautiful as ever, Eva."

"It's been a good year for us... Do you need the rest of my pack, or will I do?"

"Let's talk first. I've come for a favor and it requires action tonight. I'll need you and a few of your boys to go for a romp into town to help me take care of a certain situation."

"Really! Into town? Henry, I believe this is a first for you!" Eva was amused and intrigued. She raised her head and let out a few fun howls. Coyotes had never been asked to go near human dwellings let alone go into their community. Quite the contrary, they were forced to stay away. The punishment for going near humans could be fatal.

"Yes, and I think you'll enjoy this assignment. There's a house on the big lake, where some small, innocent animals have been imprisoned, along with a pack of wild dogs. All the animals need to be freed immediately. The men who confined them are bad people. Once we release the animals, we'll deal with the humans."

"What exactly do you want us to do, dear Henry?"

"Gather a group, four including yourself, and I'll lead you to the house. From what I've been told by my scouts, the men leave at night. We'll check out the situation, and between us we'll find a way to set the animals free. Sounds good, right Eva?"

"Dangerous is more like it. Maybe you should just show

us where to go and leave the rest to us. You can watch."

Henry let out a long sigh, "Eva, do you doubt that I'm up to the task?"

Eva sashayed over to Henry and rubbed against him. "No darling, I just don't want anything to happen to you. You know I've always had a soft spot in my heart for you."

"Okay, now you're playing with me. I am the alpha here and I will be the leader. Gather your group and let's go. Really Eva!" Then Henry laughed. She still could get the best of him, even at his age.

Eva threw back her head and let out three distinctive howls. Each howl represented the name of a member of her pack. She called Bo, Jack, and Max. Within moments three handsome, young coyotes appeared from different directions. They had been close by in case Eva needed them.

"Hi gorgeous," said Bo, a skinny brown and golden grey coyote. "We were listening. We're in. Sounds like fun and we could use a few laughs. Thanks Henry. Are there some edibles in the bunch we can bring home for breakfast?"

"Very funny Bo, you're still the kidder. The answer is NO," Henry replied, with a playful growl.

"Figured as much," crooned Jack, a handsome, steel grey, long, lean coyote.

"Come on! Are there rabbits? I like rabbits for breakfast," yipped Max, the tawny brown runt of the pack.

"Down boys, we need to behave. I promised Henry we'd just take care of business. That's what we're going to do. Got it?" Eva calmly commanded.

"Yes, my lady," Bo bowed to Eva, as did Jack and Max.

"Okay, let's go," barked Henry. The group of five headed down the mountain, through the woods, and into the far side of town.

As they made their way to town the three male coyotes kidded around. They ran, sniffed, and joked with one another. Eva and Henry stayed close together.

"Henry, I hear you have a delicious puppy grandson that's come to live with you on the farm, but where is your handsome son these days?"

"His people moved away and he had no choice but to go with them. The family didn't want Bert. Anna, my mistress, understood the situation and took the pup in, so I could have him nearby. He's an alpha, Eva, and I'm training him. He's a joy.

"Bert got roughed around pretty good today at the house we're going to. Someone they call the 'pet store guy' took a baseball bat and whacked him with it. He will have to be dealt with, too." Henry shook his head and growled.

"Oh my, I'll be happy to help. Just say the word, Henry."

"I may take you up on that, Eva."

It took the group about half an hour to run to the location of the abandoned house.

Once they reached the house, they split up to search for a way to get inside, and to make sure no humans were around. Eva was the most successful. She let out a few quick yips for the males to come to her.

Within moments, they were at her side. She had found a cellar entrance in the dirt in the backyard that led directly into the house.

"Henry look, there's light coming from underneath these doors. If we can get them open, we can get inside, and get the captured ones outside. What do you think?"

Henry agreed and relayed the order. "Come on boys get the flaps of these doors open. They're made of wood so it shouldn't take much muscle."

"Watch out Pops," Bo said and started to scratch, sniff, and study the doors. "Max, get your paw under that warped, broken piece of the wood."

Jack approached his two pals. "Guys, you know I do wood better than anyone. Get out of my way." He moved to the doors. "Yup, I can do this." He dug his teeth into the rotten wood and broke a chunk off the top. Bo and Max then put their snoots under the hole. Together they lifted the splintered wood and threw the doors open.

"Good boys," cheered Eva. "Now get out of my way! Come on, Henry. Let's see what we've got. You three stay here unless I call you. If the animals start running out, leave them alone! Stay out of their way. Oh, and mind you, there are feral dogs in there. Do not start a ruckus, or we'll all wind up in the pound."

"Eva's right," agreed Henry. "If I wind up in the pound, you'll all wind up food for the crows!"

"We got it. Call if you need us," Jack said. He was trying hard not to laugh. The three young coyotes thought

Eva and Henry were a cute pair.

While the coyotes waited, they walked down to the lake to get a drink of water. Suddenly, all hell broke loose. There was barking and meowing. A bunch of screaming animals ran out of the cellar and scattered in all directions.

The pack of dogs escaped, chasing a bunch of rabbits. The rabbits ran straight into the coyotes with the dogs right behind them. The rabbits found themselves surrounded and started squealing. The dogs stopped short because they were face to face with the coyotes. Henry came out of the cellar and barked ferociously. The rabbits dispersed unharmed and the dogs ran off. The coyotes had a good laugh and new found respect for Henry.

When all the animals were free, the coyotes closed the cellar door.

"That was crazy," howled Max.

Henry was grateful for their help. The coyotes had their fun. It was time to get out of town. Bo, Jack, and Max took off running ahead of Eva and Henry. The two old friends took their time once they reached the woods. Henry accompanied Eva home and then returned to the farm.

When Henry reached his barn, he settled into his soft bed of blankets and hay. The Lab was satisfied with their trip to town. He was content with the fact that no one would know who had set the animals free from the abandoned blue house on the big lake. As he drifted off to sleep, he thought about the earlier days when he and the beautiful Eva roamed the highline together.

CHAPTER THREE

It was now January and several inches of freshly fallen snow covered Brittany and Lace's country place. It was happy hour inside their cozy knotty pine home. The warm wood walls reflected the rich golden flames of the crackling fire that roared in the large stone fireplace in the living room. Britt and Lace were on the coffee table, a few feet away from the fireplace.

Love and Man were in the kitchen preparing appetizers and drinks and some treats to share with their cats. Love had prepared shrimp and was cutting up some small pieces for her pussycats. Man was placing cheese and crackers on a plate and would then make their cocktails.

"Love, we're in for more snow tonight," stated her husband.

"I know. I'm happy that we shopped in the city this afternoon before we traveled up here. We won't have to leave the house all weekend if we get the five to eight inches that's forecasted."

As the cats waited patiently for their treats, Brittany

leaned over to her sister and whispered, "Lace, I have to go out to the woodshed later and meet Nathanial, Henry, and a coyote named Eva.

"It turns out the wild pack of dogs Henry let out of the abandoned house are still roaming the area. We now know they are controlled by the 'pet store guy'. He feeds and houses them so they do his bidding."

"What's bidding, Britt?" asked the pretty white kitten."

"It means the dogs do whatever he asks. In this case, the man is bartering with the dogs for food and shelter." The ginger cat held up her paw. "Wait before you ask me what bartering is. It's kinda like tit for tat, trading one thing for another. The man feeds and houses the dogs, and in return they kidnap innocent animals for him to sell."

Brittany was getting good at giving Lace the answers to what words mean, even before Lace asked her. She was pleased with herself for figuring this out, because now she wouldn't have to answer all the extra questions Lace usually asked.

"Can I go with you?" asked Lace, already knowing what the answer would be.

"Not this time. The weather may be bad. It's just supposed to be a quick meeting. A plan is being put into place to deal with the 'pet store guy' and the pack of dogs. I haven't been told any details. All I know is they want me to be part of it. That's what I'm going to find out tonight.

"Wow, isn't that dangerous? I'm scared for you Brittany."

"I am too, kiddo. I've never done anything this serious

before," Britt answered and let out a deep sigh, wondering what she was going to be asked to do.

Lace instinctively hissed and puffed out. Her tail bushed and swished back and forth. "No, don't do it. I have a bad feeling. Stay out of this pleeease, Britt. Let someone else do it. Let Henry do it! He caused this when he let the dogs out. I want you safe!" The kitten hissed. Lace had once again doubled in size and now weighed close to four pounds. She was still sweet, but was also turning into a strong, fierce, young cat.

"Don't you want me to become an Elder?"

"Yes. But, not if it puts you in lots of danger."

"Danger isn't always bad. Sometimes it's actually fun. I'm a 'doer' Lace. That means I do what has to be done for the greater good. I'll have plenty of help. I'll do what I have to and come home safe, okay?"

Love came into the living room, carrying a tray, and noticed the tension between her two cats.

She placed the tray on the coffee table which held their food and drinks. She then lifted Brittany off the table into her arms and held the cat so they were face to face. "What's going on, Britt the Kit?"

While this was going on, Lace tiptoed over to the plate of shrimp, silently lifted one into her mouth, and ran away with it. Unfortunately she hadn't chosen from the plate with the cut up pieces of shrimp that Love had prepared for the cats.

Brittany relaxed in Love's arms. She enjoyed being

held, especially tonight since she was afraid of what she was going to be asked to do. She worried not only about herself, but about her family, who would suffer if anything happened to her.

After going through losing Jade, Britt understood loving and caring for someone deeply, and even though those feelings were worth it, losing someone you loved was very hard. Britt didn't want to cause her family any pain. She truly cared about Love, Man, and Lace.

Love sighed and held Brittany snug in her arms, instilling strength to her cat. "Take care Brittany, I know you're up to something."

In the meantime, Lace moved to the back of the couch and was chomping down the whole shrimp she had taken. She was eating it too quickly, feeling nervous and scared for her sister. All of a sudden, as she swallowed the last bite, her body began to shudder. 'Uh, oh, what's happening to me?' It felt like waves starting in her stomach and moving up to her throat. She started to whimper.

Love placed Britt on the table and moved quickly to the kitten. She bent down onto the rug and studied Lace's body. "What did you eat, Lace?" She then gently stroked the kitten's back and spoke in a soft voice. She moved the kitten from a rug to the wooden floor.

"Well this is another first for you. It'll be okay. You're going to throw up. It's natural, don't fight it." Lace looked up at her with hurt in her pale green eyes, then immediately threw up on the floor and looked at it with amazement.

"Brittany," she cried. "What is 'throwing up?'"

Britt trotted over to her sister. "It's what you get for gobbling up a whole shrimp. It's okay. Leave it alone, don't re-eat it, and calm down. You'll feel better in a minute."

"Wow that was serious! But you're right, I do feel better."

Love had left and returned with a wet paper towel to clean up the mess.

Man followed his wife into the room to see what happened. "So, Lace had her first barf." He bent down to the kitten, "Eat more slowly, Lace, and don't steal food!" He then swatted her behind gently.

"Okey Dokey Pops," she meowed and scampered away purring. "Brittany, that happened because I'm scared for you. DON'T GO OUT!"

Brittany was amused. "It happened because you didn't chew your food before you swallowed. It had nothing to do with me."

After that, everyone calmed down. Man turned on soft music and placed a few new logs on the fire. The flames were beautiful. The house was warm as the snow began to fall once more.

Later that night, the snow had stopped falling and the sky was clear. Brittany was asleep on the couch in the living room. The full moon was directly over one of the large skylight windows. Its brilliant light was both luminous and alarming. Britt had picked this spot on purpose. Since the sky was clear of clouds, she knew the moon's light would wake her when it was time to sneak out of the house for her meeting.

The ginger feline lowered her long neck and silently prayed, 'Earth Mother. Please let me be worthy of being an Elder like my sister Jade before me. Fill me with strength, determination, and faith so that I can be successful, and please let this tale have a happy ending. Thank you.'

After taking a few very deep breaths, Britt jumped off the couch. She made her way to the kitchen, ate some food, and took a slow drink of water. The ginger cat then went to their cat door and began to pry it open with one of her long sharp claws.

Once outside, she leaped onto the stone wall and put one paw into the snow to test its depth and softness. She needed to know if it would hold her as she made her way to the woodshed. Only a few new inches had fallen, which made the short trip manageable.

As she looked towards the shed, Brittany could see the long shadow of a large animal in the snow. When she got closer, Eva the Coyote called with a few quick yips, "Hello, I'm the only one here. Have no scent of fear as you come near."

"Easy for you to say," Britt said as she cautiously approached the coyote.

"You needn't worry. I'm Eva, Henry's friend. And, like most animals, I don't like the taste of cats. I assume you are

Britt the Kit, all grown up, strong and beautiful. Miss Jade was a great queen, and one of a very few cats that could impress or intimidate me. I have no doubt she taught you well."

Nathanial the Woodchuck popped his head out after removing a few pieces of wood in the shed that concealed the entrance to his home. "Good evening Britt and Eva."

Henry also made his appearance from the field behind the woodshed. The black Lab jumped over the stone wall and thicket bushes that ran along the back of Brittany's land. He sent out a few low woofs to announce his arrival.

The two males joined the females, and they gathered in the shed's shadow so they wouldn't be seen by any passersby.

Henry spoke first. "I must begin by taking responsibility for letting those wild dogs escape, especially, now that we know they're working for the 'pet store guy' and we realized they're still kidnapping more animals to be sold for profit. Most of those animals already had good homes or were free to live on their own."

"Henry," said Nathanial. "Your plan was a good one. It worked. You had no way of knowing the dogs were working with the 'pet store guy'. Brittany, please try and find out from your humans the man's name. He must have one. I'm tired of calling him the 'pet store guy'."

"Yes, I will Nat. I'll have it for you ASAP."

"Thank you, yes, when you get back." The woodchuck lowered his body into the snow.

"Wait a minute, where am I going?" Britt moved toward Nathanial.

Eva got between the cat and the woodchuck, "Henry will explain it to you darling."

"Don't 'darling' me Eva, just because you're a big, beautiful coyote." Britt realized she was overreacting and added. "No disrespect intended, Eva."

Eva laughed, "None taken, Brittany. She, too, lowered her body onto the snow, deferring to Henry.

"Brittany," stated Henry, "we have a plan, and this time it's extremely well thought out. We covered every possible scenario. There will be some chance involved, but we put safeguards in place to cover most of the risk."

"Excuse me! What's that supposed to mean? Henry, tell me what you want me to do, without leaving it to my imagination, because right now, the way I feel, I'm going home and locking our cat door until the dogs are caught!"

Nat moved quickly to the cat. "Britt the Kit, calm yourself. You can't think for a minute I would send you on an assignment if I thought it was too dangerous for you to handle. Miss Jade, wherever she is, would have me struck by a bolt of lightning!"

Brittany growled. "All of you, as I asked nicely before, tell me what you want me to do, NOW!"

"Guys, I wouldn't mess with her right now," whispered Eva. "Tell her, and do it quickly, before one of us feels her claws."

"Yeah, she's right," growled Britt.

"Henry, go ahead. It is a good plan and Brittany will be safe," pronounced Nathanial.

"Brittany, come here," commanded Henry. The ginger queen sat down in front of her Elder.

"Here's the plan! We're going to locate the pack of dogs and follow them to their new hideout. We believe they have captured, yet again, another batch of animals for the 'pet store guy'. Our goal is to find and release those animals and neutralize and disband the dogs. What we want, Brittany is for you to let the dogs catch you. That way we can follow and find their new location.

"Then Britt, either you'll escape and lead the dogs to us. Or if you seem to be in any danger, we'll rescue you immediately. Sky will be your partner for the night. We'll have scouts and runners ready to assist you at every turn. Either way, I will personally lead a group to get you safely home. Please know we would not ask you to do this if we didn't believe you'd succeed." Henry sat down in the snow and waited for Britt's response.

Brittany remained silent and thought about what Henry had said. She closed her eyes and went deep inside herself to check out how she really felt. Moments later she lifted her head and opened her eyes and simply said, "Okay, I'm in."

Nat, Henry, and Eva acknowledged Britt's decision and their approval by nodding their heads, followed by a big collective sigh of relief.

Lace had been listening and watching from an open window. The kitten now understood that Brittany was going on a mission. She was ready to support her. Lace was prepared to do anything she could to make sure her sister succeeded and got home safely before Love and Man woke up in the morning.

Brittany listened carefully to the details of the plan. She was pleased that Sky would be her partner, and was quite impressed with the other animals she would be working with throughout the night. When all was said and done, Britt was now confident she could 'do' what was being asked of her and would safely return to her home and family.

Sky appeared from the woods. "I've got your back Britt."

Grey-Grey slipped out of the bushes and ran to the group. "We tracked the dogs. They're not far from here. Britt, Sky, let's go!"

"I gotta let my family know…" Britt meowed.

Suddenly, a series of hisses sounded from the house. The group turned and saw Lace in the open window.

"Okay, let's go." As Britt moved towards the woods, she turned back and looked at Lace. The kitten's image was backlit by a lamp in the room where she sat in the window. Brittany warmed at the sight of her. All cats look grey in the dark. Lace's silhouette resembled Jade's.

CHAPTER FOUR

Britt, Sky, and Grey-Grey moved quickly through the woods. It didn't take long for them to join up with a few coyotes from Eva's pack. Jack and Max would stay behind, but would remain close by in case they were needed. Grey-Grey would return to the woods near Britt and Lace's land to protect their territory.

Bo, the third coyote, joined Britt and Sky and together they circled around to where the dogs were hanging out. The two cats moved into position, meowed and ran around in the snow pretending to play. This action allowed the dogs to discover them and start a chase through the woods.

Once Britt and Sky knew the dogs had seen them, they played scared and ran with the dogs hot on their tails. Bo waited until the dogs went after the cats, and then he followed the dogs.

Nathanial, Henry, and Eva had said their goodnights, moved to pre-assigned separate places to lead, and make sure everything went as planned. It was going to be a long hard night.

Lace left the window desperately trying not to panic. She ate everything she could find and took a drink of water. She tried going to bed with Love and Man, curled up and purred, trying to calm herself, but it didn't work. In less than an hour she was up and at their cat door. She gave it a push and it opened.

Lace was now convinced that she was in the right place to help her sister, so she settled down in front of the cat door to wait.

"Now I'm ready if Brittany needs me," she sighed and after a short time fell asleep.

Brittany and Sky worked well together, as always. They ran side by side, split up to tire the dogs out, and hid at one point to confuse them. They couldn't make the chase too easy, because the dogs would become suspicious. Cats were good at getting away from their predators.

After a while they met up and hid in some thicket bushes to rest. Sky sat next to his older friend. "Britt thanks for getting Scamp out of that abandoned house. It was hard to believe he could be that stupid."

"He's not stupid. Just young and inexperienced," Britt replied. "Did he tell you I made him bleed?"

"Yes, he did. We had a long talk. We're going to hang

out together more often so I can give him some pointers on staying out of trouble. He's with a scout group tonight to just observe."

"Really Sky, you think Scamp's just going to watch and not get into trouble? Spoken like a true father. Good luck with that, pal.

"Hey Sky, do you know where Bert is tonight? I hope he's part of the plan. I'm sure he'd like to get a piece of the 'pet store guy', too."

"He's not involved, Britt. I spotted Henry and Bert having a fierce argument as I was leaving the farm. They were barking, growling, and snapping at each other in the backyard of Anna's house. Henry was trying to leave and Bert kept trying to follow him. Britt, Bert lost the fight and went back to the manor house. He was angry and very upset."

"That's not fair! He's a big part of this. But I can also understand Henry's point of view. I wouldn't want Lace involved tonight either. I couldn't do what has to be done and watch out for her, too. Henry's leading all of us tonight. He can't afford to be distracted by anyone, especially Bert. He's too important to the old guy."

"Yeah, you're right. Maybe, I should have made Scamp stay home like Chayne wanted me to do. She wasn't too happy with me."

"Come on Sky, rest time is over."

Britt and Sky moved out of the bushes, purposely made some noise so that the dogs could hear them, and took off again. The cats were in tune with one another and anticipated each other's actions. It didn't take long for the dogs to hear them and pick up their scent. Once again the chase continued through the woods.

A short time later Brittany meowed and yelled, "Sky, I'm ready. I'm gonna let them catch me now. Go!"

Sky immediately ran and collided with Brittany. "No way," he said. "I'm going with you. I don't care if they told me to let you get caught by yourself. I can't just leave you and follow behind with that coyote dude Bo."

"You have to, Sky. You'll need to go back and bring the rescue group to me. Everyone knows you and they'll come with you! Bo can't do it. They'll run away from him. I'll be okay. I know you'll come right back to make sure I get out of wherever I am. Now GO! We have to follow the plan to rescue the animals and disband the dogs."

"Yes, my lady," Sky reluctantly complied. He gave Britt a body bump and ran off. He then moved to higher ground and met up with Bo. From there the tiger cat and the golden coyote could track the ginger cat's movements after she was caught by the dogs.

Brittany hid under a broken tree limb in the snow. When she heard the dogs sniffing around near her, she snapped off a small tree branch which alerted the dogs to her position. They approached her growling and snapping their teeth, with drool dripping from their mouths. Britt was now sincerely frightened and worried. The scent of her fear led one of the dogs directly to her. She went limp to show she wouldn't fight back or try to run away.

A handsome, lean, sleek, black mutt with a long fanned out tail, slowly approached the cat. His black eyes sparkled. When he showed his teeth, Brittany could see they were pearl white and razor sharp. He was a young, healthy dog. She also noticed he had a weird collar around his neck.

When he came closer, almost touching her, he said, "Stay calm, I'm undercover for SPCA. You won't be harmed. Just don't make any sudden moves. The dogs in this pack are out of control. Be cool. No one gets hurt. You'll be home by sunup."

Britt was confused. No one had told her about this undercover dog. She didn't trust him, but she had no choice except to play along. She hissed and spit at the dog, "Sorry, just playing my part. Thanks."

"My name is Jimmy," he said in a low growl. "I'm going to pick you up by the back of your neck, and carry you to our hideout." The dog moved to Britt and grabbed her with his mouth. He signaled to his buddies and they all took off.

Brittany remained quiet. She looked for scouts and landmarks so she would know where this 'Jimmy' was taking her. Sky and Bo watched Brittany being carried by the dog. Once they entered the back door of a building, the cat and coyote ran to notify Henry. He and his team, along with Sky and Bo, took off to free the animals, corner the dogs, and get Brittany home safely.

Simultaneously, Britt and Jimmy worked together to form their own plan. Jimmy placed Brittany with the captured animals. She calmly explained that help was on the way and they would all be released very soon. Jimmy lured the unruly pack of dogs into the storage room and locked them in. He then freed Brittany from the animals' room.

Britt made sure the same back door was open so Sky, Henry, and the animal rescuers could have easy access when they arrived.

Britt joined Jimmy. The undercover dog then broke off his collar, which sent an SOS signal to the Local SPCA. When the Chief of the Local SPCA received the signal he notified the police and headed off to Jimmy's location.

In the meantime, Henry and Sky showed up at the back of the building where Sky had last seen Brittany and the pack of dogs. As it turned out, the building housed a new pet store in town that was scheduled to open the following day.

Henry and Sky easily entered through a back door and found Brittany and Jimmy. Henry was quite surprised to see the black mutt. Jimmy turned out to be one of Henry's many nephews.

Henry and Nathanial had a plan in place to disband the dogs. However, after Jimmy explained his side of the story, Henry agreed to defer to the authorities. He congratulated Jimmy on a job well done.

Their timing was perfect. In the distance the sound of police sirens could be heard. The sirens alerted Henry that it was time for him to get Britt and Sky out of the store and out of town without being seen.

After Brittany thanked Jimmy for helping her, the three ran off to meet up with the rest of the rescue team waiting in the woods.

When the pack of dogs heard the police sirens, they started to howl, which caused the captured animals to start screaming. As Brittany took off with Sky and Henry, they heard the beginning of an intense uproar in the store.

As the dog and cats ran down the street, a local newspaper reporter stepped out of an all night diner across the street from the pet store. She was curious and wanted to know where the police cars were headed. The woman spotted a ginger cat heading towards the woods. She didn't notice Sky and Henry, because their dark fur blended into the shadows.

Inside the pet store's storage room, the dogs broke a window and escaped. In doing so, they set off the window's alarm. The intense blaring sound caused the dogs to freak out and sent them running for the woods, barking their heads off.

When the loud sound of the alarm went off, Jimmy headed to the room where the kidnapped animals were being held. He decided to stay with them until help arrived and hopefully calm them down.

But, when he opened the door, the animals bolted out of the room. Over twenty small frightened animals burst out of the pet store's open front door, much to the amazement of the police officers, who were just entering the store.

Jimmy wanted to run too, but knew he needed to remain

in place until the Chief of the Local SPCA showed up. He was loyal to the man. The dog sat himself down in the middle of the store and waited. Meanwhile, the local police officers turned off the alarm and searched the store, but couldn't find any people or any other animals.

Across the street, several customers from the all night diner came outside to see what was going on. Quite a few Police and Local SPCA vehicles were already parked in front of the pet store. There was a big sign on the front window announcing its grand opening the next day.

Among the group of diner customers was the proud new store owner. He was none other than the 'pet store guy'. When the sneaky man realized what was happening, he quickly moved down the street. He headed towards the woods and the sound of his barking dogs.

As he slipped away, the reporter, who was still outside, took a picture of the man with her cell phone. She immediately went looking for the Chief of the Local SPCA. Everyone in town knew the man and respected his work. The Chief, with the help of his volunteers, was famous for protecting the animals in their community.

The Chief, a large sturdy man dressed in full uniform, entered the store and found Jimmy alone and waiting for him. As the man approached his canine partner, he patted the dog's head and firmly stated, "Good work, Jimmy." He then quickly placed a new collar around the mutt's neck.

The reporter entered and observed the Chief interacting

with the dog. Lisa, the reporter, was a young woman in her thirties. She had on a black leather hat, coat, and boots. In one of her black gloved hands was her cell phone.

"Evening Chief, you need to take a look at this," she said, extending her arm to show the man the picture on her cell phone.

"What have we here?" said the Chief. When he looked at the photo, a smile formed on his face, "You just made my day, pretty lady. Did you see where the guy was headed?"

"Yes, I watched him head towards the woods where the dogs were barking. Chief, what's going on here? Can you give me a statement?"

"I'll do better than that, Lisa. You'll have an exclusive story for Sunday's local paper. Come along with us and get your story first hand."

"Great, thanks. I'll wait outside."

Once the woman had left, Jimmy barked several times and ran to the door. "Let me out of here, NOW! My assignment's not done!"

The Chief smiled, "Jimmy, wait a minute." The dog stopped and looked up at his boss. "I want you to understand, that because you led us to this location, this pet store will never open. That guy will never hurt another animal, even if I have to lock him up myself.

"Now GO! We'll be right on your tail. Find me that man, and that darn pack of dogs!" The Chief tipped his hat to the dog and let him out.

The Chief then bellowed to the police officers and

his Local SPCA volunteers, "Come on let's go! Follow that dog!" Lisa slipped into the group, right behind the Chief. They all headed towards the woods, trying to keep up with the sleek black dog.

Brittany, Sky, Henry, and his team were traveling towards the ginger cat's home. Suddenly, they heard the piercing sound of the alarm going off, followed by the sound of barking dogs. The group picked up their pace and moved quickly through the woods. The team needed to regroup and go back to their original plan to corner, capture, and disband the dogs.

When they reached a small clearing, Henry stopped and turned to his team, which included Bo, the coyote from Eva's pack. "Bo, signal Eva and your pals to round up those dogs. We'll be right behind you. If that young black SPCA dog shows up, leave him alone!"

"Yes sir. Are you sure there's just one black dog?"

"Yes, and he's my kin, so don't touch a hair on his body. You've been a great asset tonight Bo, I'm grateful. Make sure this time those dogs are cornered and can't get away."

"You got it, Henry. We coyotes like being included in the community. See ya." He was gone in an instant and all that remained were the echoes of his howl, as he called to Eva.

The stately black Lab turned his focus on Brittany. He studied the ginger cat for a moment. "Britt, what you did tonight was grand. I know it's not over yet, but you have certainly played out your part perfectly. Thank you." Henry bowed to Brittany.

From out of the woods, Nathanial the Woodchuck appeared. Brittany looked at him with admiration. He had been right. She had succeeded, once again in doing what he had asked of her. She had completed her task and was safe. The woodchuck approached the group and came to stand in front of Britt and Henry.

"Well done, Britt the Kit, who is a kit no more. You will always have that nickname. But now," Nat placed a paw on her head, "you are an Elder, and we are pleased to have you join us."

Henry stepped up and said, "We will have a proper celebration soon. But know you have proven yourself as we knew you would. He then turned to Sky, "Please see that Brittany gets home safely."

"Yes Sir. That would be an honor."

Henry and the rest of his group took off, heading to where the dogs were barking and the coyotes had begun to howl.

Nathanial remained behind and when he was alone, sighed and thought to himself... 'Life isn't as sweet without Miss Jade being here with us, but her presence, strength, and guidance does linger on. Some part of me truly believes she guided me to make sure Lace found a home with Brittany.'

CHAPTER FIVE

A few hours later, Lace woke up with a jolt, as if someone had pushed her. The white kitten sat up and looked outside. Oh no! Brittany! She's not home yet." Lace, on instinct, quietly slipped out the cat door. She jumped onto the big round dining table on the back porch and looked around. The sky was clear. The moon was starting to set and the sun was about to rise.

The kitten sniffed the air and looked around. It was quiet, too quiet. There was something disturbing in the air, but she couldn't tell what it was.

"I need help! I'm losing control of myself. Who can I call? I know!" and she called their names out loud. "NUMBER ONE, NUMBER TWO, please, I need you!"

To Lace's right, in a round circle garden, there stood a towering silver maple tree. She watched as the top limbs began to shimmer and shake.

To her left, towards the end of her property, she spotted an ash tree's branches begin to sway.

The kitten watched as a small animal made its way, running through the trees, quickly jumping from limb to limb until it reached the woodshed. Benny, the young grey squirrel with the white and grey ringed tail, jumped out of the trees onto the shed. He then leaped off the roof onto the lawn and ran towards the back porch.

Lace, didn't realize that Rikki, the grey squirrel with the white belly, had already left the silver maple tree and was next to the table where the white kitten was sitting. Lace jumped two feet in the air when a little voice asked: "What's up Lace? Why did you use the code name and call me 'One'?"

"Why didn't you announce yourself or something, Rikki? You could've given me a heart attack." Lace's heart was pounding from being so surprised.

"Hey, hi Rikki," said Benny, to his brother, when he finally stopped on the stone wall. "Lace what's the matter? It's kinda early to get us up."

"I need you here to help me if there's trouble. And to be honest I don't want to be alone. I'm worried for Brittany and I'm scared. Ever felt like that guys?"

Nodding 'yes', the squirrels jumped onto the table and sat beside their friend.

The three animals had been born around the same time that past spring and had grown up together. The squirrel brothers were happy living in the trees on Brittany and Lace's land. They were welcomed at the bird feeders, along with the birds, chipmunks, deer, turkeys, skunks, and even raccoons. Love and Man did not allow foxes, coyotes, or hawks. They were chased away, as soon as they were spotted on their land.

"I overheard," Benny said, "the conversation at the woodshed meeting earlier tonight. I also saw Brittany, your father, and Grey-Grey take off into the woods. Britt's not back yet?"

"No!" Lace hissed.

Rikki moved closer to Lace as did Benny, "We'll wait with you and help if necessary," assured Rikki.

"Okey Dokey. That makes me feel better. Thanks! It's good to have neighbors like you." Lace took a deep breath, settled down between her friends, and waited.

The moon moved closer to the mountain ridge. The stars were beginning to disappear as the sun's light faintly spread across the sky. In the distance, the three young animals heard dogs barking. Their barks sounded frantic and they were moving closer.

Lace bolted from the table and quickly ran across the snow into the woods. The squirrels followed and once in the woods they each climbed a tree on either side of where Lace had stopped. Now they not only heard barking dogs, but men yelling, too.

Benny yelled to Lace, "Climb up here with us!"

"No! I'm not good at climbing trees," called the white kitten. The squirrels could barely see her in the snow.

"Lace, if someone comes just burrow deep into the snow

and shut your eyes. You'll be invisible!" called Rikki.

"Good idea, thanks," the kitten replied. Lace settled down into the snow, and closed her green eyes.

Not far away, Brittany and Sky moved quickly through the dark woods. They were now getting closer to the ginger cat's home. "Sky, I don't know about you, but I got a bad feeling in my gut."

"Me too, Britt the Elder, maybe we should both go up into the trees until the sun comes up."

"Really, you're not going to call me that, are you?"

"No, but I wanted to acknowledge it. I think it's great. It's natural for me to think of you that way. I've looked up to you since you saved my life."

"Good and thanks. I guess it will take me time to get used to it. But right now, Sky, I'm too exhausted to climb. I need to rest before we go any further. You go check the area for both of us. Just let me know if I need to run. Go on, Sky. I'll be fine." Brittney lowered herself to the ground. The cat was both bone tired and chilled to her core.

"Okay, I'll head up a tree and have a look around. Stay put. Eat some snow. I've got you covered."

Sky climbed up a tall maple tree and surveyed the surrounding area. There was only enough light in the sky to see shadows. His intense blue eyes scanned the dark woods.

Benny spotted the black and white tiger cat climbing a huge tree. He called to Rikki and Lace. "There's a cat in a tree just north of here."

Rikki looked and recognized the cat. "It's Sky! It's your father, Lace!"

Lace opened her eyes and meowed to Sky, "Papa, what are you doing here? Where is Brittany? Is she safe? Pleeease tell me!"

"Lace, get out of here," commanded Sky. "Go home. Brittany is with me, and yes, she's safe. No! Wait! Stay there. Someone's moving through the woods and heading your way." As Sky again scanned the area, he saw a quick flash of movement in the snow. He could not believe his eyes. "Scamp! Son, what are you doing here? Go help Lace. Both of you, quickly, hide in the snow!"

Lace was looking for a good place to hide, when she heard Sky screaming again. She stopped, looked around, and spotted her brother. "Scamp, I'm over here!"

Scamp ran to his sister. "Hey Lace, what are you doing out of your house?" Scamp was so calm. Lace knew he didn't have a clue about the danger that was surrounding everyone.

"SSScamp, what are you doing here?" The kitten hissed at her brother.

"I'm observing. What a night. It's crazy out there."

"You're a mess, you know that, right? Don't you realize that we're in danger?" The two kittens were so busy fussing with one another that they were unaware that someone was sneaking up on them. It was none other than the 'pet store guy'.

Rikki and Benny tried to warn Lace and Scamp by

screeching and yelling, but the kittens weren't paying attention. Frustrated, the squirrels took off flying through the trees to get help.

Sky didn't see the man until he had already reached down and grabbed Lace and Scamp. There was nothing he could do. He froze and held his breath.

Lace and Scamp felt themselves being roughly grabbed and lifted off the ground. They screamed, hissed and spit, as they struggled to get free, releasing an awful odor that cats let off when they feel threatened.

When they realized, at the same moment, who had captured them, their eyes locked on each other with the same thought...'It's the 'pet store guy'!' The time had finally come to get even with the guy that kidnapped their litter and Bert and all the animals that had become victims of his acts of cruelty. Scamp winked at Lace and they went limp in the man's hands.

As the man loosened his grip, the white kitten twisted around and bit down hard on the man's thumb. The man screamed in pain and dropped her in the snow. Scamp wiggled out of the man's other hand, and ran up his arm, digging sharp claws through the man's clothes and scratching his skin. The tiger kitten then scampered up and bit the man's ear. Pleased with himself, he dug his claws into the man's exposed neck. When the man tried to grab him, Scamp ran down his back into the snow.

As her brother hit the snow, Lace started up the man's

leg on his other side, penetrating his pants with her intense, super-sharp, curved claws. When she reached his belt, he turned and tried to grab her. Scamp, meanwhile, had climbed a tree. He dove onto the man's back and dug his claws in deep.

All in all, Lace and Scamp were doing their worst, enjoying finally getting even with this guy. The man swung around trying to get Scamp off his back, only to discover Grey-Grey the fox, poised in front of him. The man didn't move a muscle. The kittens retreated and jumped into the snow.

The grey fox looked into the man's eyes and let out a low deep growl, followed by a couple of nasty barks. The 'pet store guy' took off, yelling for help, tripping and falling over branches and rocks as he ran through the woods.

Lace and Scamp ran to the fox, thankful and meowing with every ounce of their being, "WE DID IT!"

Grey-Grey stared in awe at the two brave kittens standing before him. Then he shook his head and said, "Yes, you did, you crazy little kittens. Now, Scamp, get back to the farm before your father sees you again. Lucky for you two I was nearby and Rikki and Benny came to get me."

"Yes Sir, thank you." Scamp replied very sincerely. Then he turned to his sister. "Lace, you were awesome. You puffed out to twice your size and fought like a true queen. I'm going home to Ma, so she can protect me from Pops. Take care." The tiger cat was gone in a flash.

Lace now looked up at Grey-Grey. The fox stared down at her sternly.

"Uh oh, hi, how are you?" asked the frazzled white kitten, not knowing what else to say.

"Very cute, Sugar. May I ask, WHAT ARE YOU DOING OUT HERE!?"

"I was going to hide, like my Papa said. Hey, wait a minute, you called me Sugar."

Lace looked up at the fox and finally understood who Grey-Grey was. He had called her by her secret name. Lace then remembered her Mama Chayne's words: 'Only a few will know you by the name Sugar. And, when they do, my darling, know that you can trust them with an open heart.'

"Yesss!" Lace now hissed sweetly.

"Finally, she gets it. I'm your protector, not your enemy. May I escort you home now, my young queen?"

"Oh, that would be wonderful, thank you. Will you carry me or should I run?" For the first time that night, Lace felt safe. She meekly approached the fox.

"You are something else. Come over here." The kitten ran to the fox and allowed him to pick her up by the back of her neck. He carried her swiftly to her cat door and gave her an affectionate swat on her backside as she scooted inside the cat door.

As the fox started to leave, he glanced up at the window in the kitchen door and froze when he saw Love staring at him. She looked at him with piercing green eyes, but the smile on her lips conveyed a warm thank you. Grey-Grey nodded 'you're welcome' and ran to the woods.

Love turned around and looked at Lace sitting behind her. The woman then sat herself down on the floor, crooked her finger, and gently called, "Come to me, Lace." The kitten hesitated for moment, and then ran into her arms so fast and hard that she knocked the woman over and landed on her chest.

Once Sky knew that Lace was home and Scamp was heading back towards the farm, he returned to Brittany who had fallen into an exhausted sleep.

"Wake up, Britt the Kit, I'm back and all is well. You were right about Scamp, he couldn't stay away from the action, and neither could Lace. They were both in the woods. They had quite a time for themselves."

Brittany was instantly alert. "Are they safe? Is Lace home? What happened?"

"They were nabbed by the 'pet store guy' but they are both fine. They worked together to get free of his grasp and then attacked the guy. First, I was scared, and then mad, but then it was almost comical to see Lace and Scamp go ballistic on the guy with their claws and teeth. I gotta tell ya Britt, they were impressive."

"That's awesome, Sky! You're sure they're okay?"

"Yes, Grey-Grey showed up and gave the 'pet store guy' a run for his kibbles."

"Purrfect. Listen, the woods are quiet. Is it over?"

"Yes Brittany, I think it is. From the tree I was able to

see our group saying their goodbyes and returning to their homes. I also saw Jimmy with the Chief and the woman who was dressed in black that spotted you on our way out of town. They had the 'pet store guy' and were in the process of handing him over to the police. The pack of dogs was being loaded onto a transport van. Your mission was successful Brittany. Well and truly done."

"Thanks, Sky. I wouldn't have succeeded without you as my partner. I think I'd like to go home now. I need Love's arms around me and I need to see that Lace is okay. Will you see me home?"

"As you wish..." Sky bowed to the brave queen.

Sky watched as Brittany made her way from the edge of the woods to the back door of her home. He waited until Love let her in the house.

He then headed home to the farm and his family. He planned to check in with Henry. Then he'd head home to have a few words with Scamp. Finally, he'd find Chayne to help lick his wounds. It had been a long hard night, as Nathanial said it would be, but it was now over. The woods were quiet and Sky could feel the warmth of the sun on his back as it rose over the mountains.

Lace spotted her sister looking in through their cat door. The kitten squealed and meowed, "Brittany! You're home!" Love looked too, and saw Britt peering in from the other side of the door. She immediately put the kitten on the floor and opened the kitchen door. Britt ran in.

As Love locked both doors, she was both curious and frustrated. "I know I locked these doors last night. Never mind," she muttered to herself. "They're home. That's all that matters."

"Brittany," Love called, "please come to me. I want to make sure you're not hurt and I need to hold you in my arms."

When Britt came into the kitchen, Love was amazed by her demeanor. Even though her cat was smeared with mud, soaking wet, and chilled to the bone, with pieces of debris from the woods stuck in her fur, she looked extremely pleased with herself and all grown up. She seemed different, in a good way. Love could tell the night had transformed her. She appeared somehow larger and older, and somehow noble. Love couldn't put her finger on exactly what it was, but she knew Brittany was satisfied with the outcome of the night's events.

Lace approached her sister, sniffed her, and then lovingly began to lick and clean her face. "What happened, Brittany?"

Britt looked down at Lace. "I'll tell you everything in the morning, promise. But for now, don't react, I became an Elder tonight."

Lace's eyes got very large and so green, but the kitten kept herself under control and was very cool. "I knew you could do it!" Lace purred and worked even faster to clean her sister's face.

Love took a deep breath and smiled at the sight of her

girls. They were now bonded to one another and that made her happy. Brittany was not the first cat she'd lived with, and certainly not the last, that would come back from some sort of adventure and was lucky to have made it home. But, Love decided for now, she would tend to Britt and Lace's needs. Then, when the sun was up in an hour or so, she could make some calls and find out what had happened in the area during the night.

CHAPTER SIX

It was Sunday night, at the end of the long snowy weekend. Love, Man, Brittany, and Lace would be heading back to New York City in the morning. At the moment, in their country home, there was a lovely warm fire burning in the fireplace. Love was in the kitchen putting up their dinner.

Man was waiting for her on the living room couch, scanning the front page headlines of the local Sunday paper. One headline in particular caught his attention. He couldn't believe his eyes! There was a picture of the Chief of the Local SPCA, a young black mutt, and a disheveled man who appeared to have several red scratch marks on his head and neck. His clothes were covered with dirty snow, mud, and debris from the woods. The headline read:

Local SPCA Chief, SPCA Volunteers and Local Police Track Down and Arrest Pet Store Owner

After Love was settled on the living room couch across from the fireplace, Man leaned over to her and said, "Love, I'd like to read you a very interesting front page article. I believe it will answer all your questions about the events of the other night and our darling cats."

"Okay," she responded. "There's time before dinner's ready."

Man began to read...

"In today's early morning hours, pet store owner Owen Sylvester was arrested for Acts of Cruelty, kidnapping, and the illegal sale of local animals. In addition, authorities apprehended a pack of dogs that had been wreaking havoc in the area over the last few weeks. Police records show that this was not Mr. Sylvester's first offense. He had been fined last spring when he was arrested and his pet store in the center of town closed for similar crimes.

The Local SPCA Chief stated, "This time he's not getting off with just a fine," and he added, "I will make sure this 'pet store guy' will never again be trusted with the care or sale of domestic animals. His treatment of said animals caused them to be malnourished and sick. He then knowingly put these animals up for sale to unsuspecting citizens. He is due in court Monday morning at 9AM."

The Chief was ably assisted by a well-trained, black mutt named Jimmy.

The young mutt discovered the crime scene

location and alerted the Chief, touching off the investigation and the pet store owner's arrest. A ginger cat was also spotted leaving the location moments before the authorities arrived."

When Man finished reading, he showed his wife the headline and the picture. Love took a look. Her green eyes scanned the picture.

"That's the 'pet store guy' from the store where we found Lace, Scamp, Coco, Willa and Bert!

It may sound crazy, but we were drawn to that store because I insisted on a white kitten. Remember, when I fell in love with the painting in Joanne's kitchen? It was of a young girl holding a white cat, and I got chills, and knew at that moment, our next cat would be pure white. Then, last spring, Marge's phone call led us to the exact pet store where we found Lace.

"Yes," Man was intrigued.

"Was that a coincidence or was it destiny? And, because of that, we were able to save her and the rest of the animals from that horrible place.

Man was thoughtful, "That's hard to say." Then he laughed, "And, I suppose the ginger cat mentioned in the paper was our very own Britt the Kit? Hey, maybe it was Lace and her brother Scamp, who scratched up the 'pet story guy' in the woods."

"Maybe..." Love laughed, too. Then she picked up a pillow from the couch and threw it at her husband's head.

"So where are our girls? It's time for dinner." Man called to the back of the house: "Britt, Lace, come here, please."

His voice could be heard throughout their cozy home.

The cats were stretched out in the big bed of the master bedroom, relaxing and listening to Love and Man's conversation. When they heard Man calling, Lace looked at her sister questioningly.

"Uh oh," whispered Lace. "They figured it out, now what do we do?"

"They think they know, but can't really know, understand?"

"No," Lace sat up.

"They're putting pieces of the story together... We know Man got the paper at the end of the driveway after the snow plough came through. Nathanial told me this afternoon there would be an article in the local newspaper. He said that Jimmy, the Local SPCA dog, was in the picture with the 'pet store guy' and the Chief. And, that the reporter said a ginger cat was spotted leaving the pet store moments before the police showed up. They can only suspect it was me.

As for you and Scamp, their spin on this tale is true, but it came from Man's imagination. As far as you're being destined to spend your life with us, we now know that was meant to be. It was and is your destiny. Thank goodness Nathanial got you here."

"Okey Dokey, Britt the Elder, so now what do we do?" Lace meowed.

"Very funny, I told you not to call me that. Let's go have dinner and confirm their spin on our tale. It should be fun."

"Hey Britt, by the way you were right about what Jade taught you."

"About what?"

"Remember, about being careful what you wish for. Well, I learned that lesson the hard way, too. And, you were also right about danger, it can be fun. Getting even with the 'pet store guy' was fun in a scary way, and Scamp and I lived to tell the tale!"

The cats bolted off the bed and ran to the living room. They jumped onto the coffee table and sat there like two furry angels.

"So, did the two of you have anything to do with this?" Man said, with mock seriousness, and shook the newspaper around in the air. The cats scattered and their folks broke out laughing.

Meekly the cats returned to the table. Love and Man sat on the couch, waiting for their response. Brittany and Lace then meowed as their heads moved up and down in unison.

Lace meowed... "Yesss, it was me and Scamp that got even with the 'pet store guy'!"

Brittany meowed... "Yes, it was me leaving town. And, I've become an Elder like Jade!"

"Well," Man smiled and said, "Looks like this tale has a happy ending."

Love reached for Brittany and Man picked up Lace. The cats purred and snuggled onto their laps. Brittany and Lace would have many adventures together. Brittany would love, protect, and always take care of Lace. The white kitten and the ginger cat had truly become sisters.

-The End Of This Sweet Tale-

We hope you enjoyed this book.

Here is a peak at Book One in the Sweet Tales Series.

SWEET TALES

THE ADVENTURES OF
MISS JADE & BRITT THE KIT

TONY NEEDS A FRIEND

CHAPTER ONE

Jade's round green eyes followed Venice the Pigeon as he flew away. The pretty Russian Blue cat didn't know her younger sister, Brittany, was sitting behind her on the terrace of their family's apartment high above New York City.

"What were you and that pigeon talking about?" asked Brittany, an orange and white tabby kitten.

"Nothing that concerns you, Britt," Jade replied, as she turned her attention to the kitten, who had been adopted six months earlier by their humans, Love and Man. The pigeon's news was upsetting and Jade had neither the time nor patience to answer her questions.

"Tell me! Please…" Brittany whined. "He's just an old, fat smelly pigeon. I'm your loyal, fun-loving, very gorgeous own Britt the Kit. Loved and adored by all who know me."

"Very funny," Jade playfully growled. "Go away or I'll hurt you. And don't be nasty. Venice is a legend in Manhattan."

"He doesn't look like one."

"You little brat," Jade leaped at the kitten.

Now Brittany was happy. She had Jade's attention. The two cats ran through their spacious sunny apartment. Jade chased Britt over and under furniture, in and out of closets and rooms. "They were having a wonderful time when they collided with Man.

"What have we here?" Man said looking down at the cats piled at his feet. Jade stepped away. Brittany meowed and allowed herself to be picked up and hugged. "Was she chasing you? Poor kitten. You can have a treat."

After following them into the kitchen and sharing Brittany's tuna, Jade found a quiet place on the terrace to think and bathe. She jumped onto a pillowed lounge chair, sniffed the air, stretched from head to tail, and circled several times before laying down.

When she was settled, she recalled Venice's words: "There is a boy named Tony. He is frightened and lonely. I don't know how to help him. He is not fond of birds."

While Jade pondered this problem, she used her long pink tongue to wet down one of her front paws.

Her silky, blue-grey fur resembled Pussy Willow buds, her favorite nickname. She used the wet paw to make small circles and clean around her mouth and nose. Her eyes opened and closed with the smooth motion. Soon the circles became bigger and moved over her eyes and ears.

Jade thought about the boy's sad circumstances. Tony's father had become very sick in the middle of the night a few weeks ago. He was rushed away by ambulance. Jade remembered the night because everyone on their street heard the sirens from the ambulance and police car.

Since that night, Venice told Jade, Tony and his Mom were miserable. "Strangers go in and out of the house. Some bring food. Others stay with Tony when his Mom goes out, and often whisper and sometimes weep. Tony tries to retreat to the backyard or his room but he can't seem to avoid clashing with the grownups."

Jade had felt Venice's anger. "And his Mom has no time for the boy. Not even a smile. She's either out, or yelling, or crying, or talking on the phone. Tony is quite alone and worried about his Dad."

Jade paused and squinted into the sun's light. "He needs a friend," she said softly. I've got to find a way to get to him. "I've got to do it without getting caught, or Brittany knowing. I haven't time to satisfy her curiosity."

The smell of coffee drifted onto the terrace. Its scent told Jade milk was around. She jumped from the chair and joined Brittany and Love in the kitchen.

"Good morning, girls," Love said to her cats. Brittany meowed and rubbed against her leg. Jade sat patiently.

"The milk is fresh. You can both have some." She filled two saucers with milk and placed them next to the cats' food bowls.

Brittany took a few licks of the cold white liquid. "You can have mine, Jade. I'm out of here."

As Jade finished the milk, Brittany ran to the terrace.

"Wow! It's a pretty day." She slipped through a tiny

opening to the neighbor's adjoining terrace. Once she was on the other side, the kitten was in her own world.

As Brittany looked north, perched on the 18th floor of the Upper East Side building, she was fascinated and frightened by what she saw and heard.

She watched the endless flow of traffic traveling down Second Avenue toward the heart of the city. She followed the sounds of emergency sirens as they raced around the city. Trucks thundered as they moved forward and beeped when they backed up, and there was the continual grinding noise of garbage trucks. She heard children yelling to one another on their way to school. The voices of people filtered upward as they went about their business on the sidewalks below.

Brittany's gaze left the streets and moved to the rooftops of the tenement buildings that stretched for several blocks below her. She saw men working. Teenagers kissed, thinking they couldn't be seen. On a school building, children played atop a screened-in roof.

"When the kitten looked higher, her golden eyes squinted at high-rise apartment buildings that soared into the sky, some reaching 40 stories. She spotted helicopters and planes as they traveled north along the Hudson River, making a right turn high above Harlem, heading east toward LaGuardia Airport.

"It must be great to fly," she said, watching a bird circle and then fly towards her. It was the same pigeon. She hid behind a potted plant as Venice swooped down and landed on the rail.

"Miss Jade," Venice called. "Please. Come out." His head bobbed up and down nervously. "What can we do for Tony?"

Jade appeared and said with certainty, "I'm coming out."

"But how?" Venice asked.

'How, and why?' Brittany wondered. 'She can't get out of here.' She lay down quietly and listened.

Jade, not knowing Britt was around, spoke openly. "Rose, our housekeeper will be here soon. I've decided to venture out in the laundry basket."

"Will you be safe, Miss Jade?"

"Time will tell, Venice. Can you wait for me in the backyard of this building?"

"Yes, but…"

"Good. Now, I have to get out without Brittany knowing."

"I don't think you can," said a little voice.

"Venice, why didn't you tell me she was over there?"

"Sorry old friend, I didn't see her." The pigeon poked his head around the divider and spotted the kitten sitting next to the plant. "You must be Britt the Kit. I'm Venice the Pigeon."

"How did you know to call me that?"

"Because it is your nickname." Venice flew down and landed near Brittany. They were the same size.

"If you come closer, I'll attack you," Brittany hissed.

"Will you now?" Venice eyed her carefully.

Brittany suddenly felt timid.

Venice was stunned by the flash of orange that ran past

him as Brittany ran to Jade.

"You can't get out," she cried.

"Yes, I can. Now go inside," Jade purred.

"Listen to Miss Jade," said Venice. He tried shooing her into the apartment with his open wings. Brittany arched her back and puffed in protest. Suddenly, the tumblers to the front door lock clicked open.

"It must be Rose!" Jade said.

"Time to fly. I'll be waiting, Miss Jade." Venice disappeared.

"Brittany, will you help me?"

"But I'm scared for you." Brittany touched Jade's nose.

"Well," said Rose, "if that isn't the cutest thing." The cats meowed and ran toward the older woman. "How are my girls today?" They purred and rubbed against her leg. "I love you too. We'll play later. I've got work to do." She left the room.

"Brittany, please listen to me! Quick as you can, run to the bedroom, jump onto the bed and stop Rose from taking off the sheets. I need time to hide."

"But Jade, you can't. What will happen if you get hurt? Who's gonna help you?" the kitten cried.

"GO! And don't worry. You can watch me from the bedroom window." Jade patted Brittany's behind. The kitten did as she was told.

When Jade was alone she lowered her head and whispered a prayer. "Please Earth Mother, I need your help and extra power for my journey." Silent and still, she waited for strength and determination to fill her. Slowly she lifted her head and took in as much air as her body could hold, then slowly let it out. "It's time. I do hope this tale has a happy ending."

31441251R00109

Made in the USA
Middletown, DE
30 April 2016